DILYS ROSE was born and brought ... been her home for many years. Prev... collections of short stories, *Our ...* *Tides* and *War Dolls*, three of po...

Thing, Madame Doubtfire's Dilemma and *Lure,* and a novel, *Pest Maiden.* She has also written for stage and collaborated with musicians and visual artists. Awards include the first Macallan/ *Scotland on Sunday* Short Story Prize, The RLS Memorial Award, The Society of Authors' Travel Award, The Canongate Prize and two Scottish Arts Council Book Awards. *Red Tides* was short-listed for both the McVitie's Scottish Writer of the Year and the Saltire Scottish Book of the Year. *Pest Maiden* was nominated for the IMPAC Prize. She teaches creative writing at Edinburgh University. For more information visit www.dilysrose.com

By the same author

Fiction:
Selected Stories (Luath, 2005)
Pest Maiden (Headline Review, 1999)
War Dolls (Headline Review, 1998)
Red Tides (Secker & Warburg, 1993)
Our Lady of the Pickpockets (Secker & Warburg, 1989)

Poetry:
Lure (Chapman, 2003)
Madame Doubtfire's Dilemma (Chapman, 1989)
Beauty is a Dangerous Thing (Top Copy, 1987)

For Children:
When I Wear my Leopard Hat (Scottish Children's Press, 1997)

Lord of Illusions
and other stories

DILYS ROSE

Luath Press Limited

EDINBURGH

www.luath.co.uk

First published 2005

The paper used in this book is recyclable.
It is made from low-chlorine pulps produced in a low-energy,
low-emission manner from renewable forests.

The publisher acknowledges subsidy from the Scottish Arts Council

 Scottish
Arts Council

towards the publication of this volume.

Printed and bound by
Bookmarque Ltd, Croydon

Typeset in 10.5 point Sabon
by Jennie Renton

For Lynn & Moyna

Acknowledgements

Some of these stories have previously been published in *TLS Stories*, *Borderlines* (Mainstream), *Damage Land* (Polygon), *Outlandish Affairs* (Luath), *Once upon our time: Portrait Miniatures by Moyna Flannigan* (National Galleries of Scotland), *The Times Literary Supplement*, *InScotland*, *Nerve*, *Mslexia*, *Sandstone Review*, *Scottish Book Collector*, *The Sunday Herald* and *The Herald*.

Thanks to Moyna Flannigan for providing visual inspiration for the stories, 'Lord of Illusions', 'I'm a Stranger Here Myself' and 'See You in Shangri-la', to David Wilson for his knowledge of horse racing, to Peter Clandfield, Martin Belk, Lynn Ahrens, Fiona Elliott, Gerald Mangan, Françoise Pinteaux-Jones, Helen Dunwoodie, Brian McCabe and Jennie Renton.

The author would like to acknowledge Scottish Arts Council support during the period of writing this collection.

Contents

Misha

AFTER ONLY A few days back on earth, he felt an unbearable desire to float. His girlfriend Valentina was supposed to meet him at the reception ceremony but had been called away suddenly to attend to her dying mother and, though he understood her responsibilities, gravity pained him. Like all cosmonauts, his muscles had atrophied after a spell in space and though he had diligently applied himself at the gym for the recommended number of hours each day, he was still gasping for it; for weightlessness. Had she not been at her mother's deathbed, Valentina might have distracted him from his craving to return to the womb-like existence inside the spacecraft. The team had been given a heroes' welcome – the best champagne and vodka that money could buy, Beluga caviar, spit-roasted wild boar and all the bombastic speeches anybody could stomach, in spite of the fact that the mission had made no significant discoveries and the team had hated each other from liftoff. But without gravity anchoring his feet to the frosty St Petersburg street, how light, how free, how unborn he'd felt.

Lord of Illusions

JUST AFTER DAWN, on the morning of the meet in his home town, Damon O'Fee looked in the washroom mirror and saw, behind his own reflection, the dark silhouette of a horse's head. He turned to the window and looked out through a mesh of spider webs, spatters of mud. Nothing but turf beaded with dew in the bluish first light. He'd have heard a horse, had there been one, its snorts and snuffled plumes of steamy breath, its hooves sucking on soft ground or knocking off hard. There was no mistaking a horse. He knew the stables were still closed but also knew what he saw.

When he turned back to the mirror all it held was his own coquettish reflection. What he'd seen, what he thought he'd seen must have been some spilling over of dream. The previous night, as always before a race, he'd dreamed a jumbled kind of action preplay. Most of it had already slipped away but there was still something hanging around about a horse refusing at the stalls. It didn't spook him. Damon wasn't the kind to get spooked before a race. Nervous, yes but a bit of edge was good.

He blinked, splashed his face with cold water. He was pleased with his hair colour, a glossy pheasant red he'd applied the night before and left on three times as long as the bottle recommended. His gran would like it. Remind her of the bright mop of curls he had as a boy which, by the time he hit puberty, turned limp and muddy. His gran would like the silks he'd be wearing too. She'd a preference for patterns – and today he'd be wearing the diabolo, the red stars on purple, the brown spots on cream – the chocolate buttons, as she insisted on calling them. He rubbed his neck, massaging his collarbone which still ached in the mornings from a fall. This would be his first race for three weeks. Home turf. For better or worse.

As the van began its slow descent and the town slid into view, the river, catching the morning sunlight, shone solid and inert. Damon saw, not water but shackles of steel twisting through the cobbled, historic heart of the place. It had city status now but for him, it would always be a town, a town he'd turned his back on for long enough. One which had turned its back on him for longer. Apart from his gran there was only one person he might want to see, one person he might want to be seen by, as he cracked down the track and, if Lady Luck was with him, brought in a winner.

The radio was tuned into the racing news and the two other older jocks in the van, Reg Bisley and Flannan Kale, exchanged cynical quips about the predictions with Johnny Bung, stable boy and today's driver. Bisley had a favourite in Uncle Max, Sherbet Lad was a likely place for Kale. But whatever either of them did today, the older men were hanging in there by their nails. Damon had age on his side. He ignored the banter and scanned the streets, choked with traffic and clutters of dithering pedestrians, on the lookout for a slight brisk body, a shock of crow-black hair. Three times his heart skipped a beat but, on closer inspection, two targets of Cupid's arrow turned out to be Japanese tourists, the third a girl Goth with a mess of metal studding her face.

Han would be working. Or nipping round to the bookie's.

Damon knew from his gran that since he had taken over the Great Wall from his uncle, who'd had a stroke, Han worked hard and gambled hard. Preferred poker but still gave the gee-gees a share of the restaurant profits. Would he show for the meet? Damon reckoned Han could get away if a horse took his fancy. Or a jock. To see him on the street, watch him pass by unawares, on an errand. That impatient sashay. Those neat feet. It had been a while. Too long. Not long enough. No way of telling which.

The road to the racetrack was littered with pheasant, living dangerously or already having succumbed to their fate, tail feathers splayed on the road like tribal headdresses after a massacre. Stupid birds; badly designed. Walking liabilities. But in spite of plump bodies, short legs and long, impractical tails, they could run when they felt like it. Only trouble was, they had a habit of running towards an oncoming vehicle. Johnny Bung was going on about bumping off a brace and roasting them over a campfire. Damon didn't bother explaining that there was more to game than scraping it off the tarmac.

He glanced at his partial reflection in the wing mirror, checking his new hair colour again. In broad daylight it was brighter than the pheasants' plumage, blazing. But vanity didn't obliterate the way he felt. Which was hungry. Hungry enough to eat roadkill. And would stay hungry until after the races, the final weighing-in and the walk to his gran's. He couldn't imagine ever getting used to the hunger. When his stomach began growling loudly enough to compete with the radio, Bisley and Kale started chewing over the food issue in the tiresome, blasé way of old-timers, each claiming they'd got it covered, learned to live without any interest in eating. Bisley was grey and lean as a whippet but Kale had the boiled lobster cheeks of someone who spent hours in the sauna, sweating off unwanted ounces and pounds.

Sometimes Damon got into the self-denial, the buzzy lightheadedness of it, the burning in the gut close to a turn-on but today he was hallucinating food: strips of crispy duck, scallions spliced into green and white tails for spreading hoisin sauce over the pancakes Han had made at the speed of light, kneading the dough with the lightness of touch he'd given, later, to Damon's fourteen-year-old body. Pale as pancake dough, Han had whispered in his ear as he licked and bit. In the dining room, Han's uncle had snored at a table set up for dinner: straw place mats, disposable chopsticks in paper wrappers and wine glasses stuffed with napkins folded to look like lotus flowers. Later, up on the hill at the outskirts of town, the two boys hung over the edge of the cliff and looked down on the sinuous contours of their world.

After the first couple of races – in which Damon's horses came in sixth out of eight runners and seventh out of eleven, the sun emerged from behind a blanket of dark cloud with a sudden blast of heat. The punters were smiling under their panama hats as the jocks made their parade from the weighing room to the paddock where the saddled horses were being walked round. Damon had a good look at his last mount of the day. Number seven. Lord of Illusions. The colt wasn't taking kindly to being paraded: frisking and skittering, snickering and fussing with the bit, keen to get moving. Beside the glossy bays, he didn't look like much: a blue roan with a skinny, veiny neck and straying, edgy eyes – a slum boy. The fleur-de-lys shaved on his rump was an attempt at a bit of class but on him it was more like a tattoo.

Damon could see contempt on the punters' faces as the lad walked him round, trying but failing to settle him. And when the trainer, Toby Saltcoats, tried to whisper sweet nothings in his twitching ears, he was worse than ever, like a hyper kid playing up in front of a parent. Tobs was togged up for the hot summer day in a sand-coloured linen suit. He was none too pleased when the horse dribbled on his jacket but kept the capped smile on his face in case anybody was looking. Which of course plenty were, that's what they were there for, to size up the horses and the jocks, and pass their verdict.

The parade was bad enough, half-way between meat market and catwalk, the men muttering about weight, the women braying about the colours they liked and the cute boys wearing them. At least the jocks only had five minutes in the paddock, time to shake hands with trainers and any owners who showed up, time to exchange pleasantries and reassurances before the bell rang and they could saddle up and head out to the track.

The canter down to the starting post didn't settle Illusions at all and the sight of the stalls had him rearing and shying. Nothing for it but the blindfold, though Damon had little faith in the calming effect on a nervous creature of its world going suddenly dark and four pairs of unfamiliar hands pushing it into a metal cage. While the back gates were shut and the blindfold removed, Damon stole a quick glance towards the stand. Sure enough there it was, in the second front row, the chocolate button brolly which matched his colours, protecting his gran's wrinkly old face from the sun. She'd have her betting slip clutched in the other hand. £2 on Lord of Illusions. At 14–1. His gran always bet on his horse, even when he warned her it didn't have a chance.

– Gambling is part sense and part stupidity, she'd say. Which suits me fine.

Damon was relieved to see the brolly. Nothing would have kept his gran from being there but she was slow on her feet and sometimes, if she left her bet until the last minute, didn't always make it back in time for the start of the next race. At least there was one person out there to cheer him on, not that he reckoned there'd be any reason to cheer. And if there was anybody else out there rooting for him, he might never know. Han also had his pride.

The horses poured out of the stalls, The Lord lagging at the start but not for long. Once they were round the first bend he gradually began to make up lost ground, edging towards then through the bunch hugging the rail, muscles rippling like lava, gaining on the leaders at the final turn, making steady headway down the final furlong without even a flick of the stick. All Damon had to do was hold on. And while he held on, instead of seeing the rising, roaring crowd in the stand, and hearing the pounding hooves and the crack of sticks around him, he saw Han, looking up from folding napkins. Han but not Han. He was wearing blinkers, black leather with red trim. His broad, smooth face had narrowed and lengthened, pointed velvety ears shot up through his hair, lips snickered back to reveal a horsey set of choppers.

– That scraggy nag had us all fooled, grunted Bisley, slapping Damon's shoulder.

– Didn't need much help from you, boy, yelled Kale. Could've stuck a fucking saddlebag in your place.

Damon had to read the names on the screen to believe he'd won the race. He had no recollection of the home stretch at all, nothing but Han as a horse, and when a girl in a horrible flowery dress lumbered up, introduced herself as Fenella Basingstoke and shoved a mike under his nose, he had no words to describe his victory other than the tired old standby he'd sworn he'd never trot out:

– It was just like a dream, Fenella.

– A dream, Damon – don't you mean an illusion?

Behind the winners' stand a couple of women in hats chortled.

When he came out of the weighing room, dressed for off, his gran waved her rolled-up brolly at him in greeting and continued nattering to Bisley and Kale, quizzing them about their diet and training, their long and now limping careers on the turf. She even had the brass neck to venture into queries about their love life. Kale had been fine. He'd had a poor day, nothing more than fourth in one race but his gran's wittering admiration of all things jockey – so strong, so brave, so hard-working, such discipline, such a lovely colourful sight, always a hit with the ladies – brought out the gallant in him. Kale could be a right cunt when he felt like it. Bisley, who'd done best out of the three of them – two winners and a second, all with prize money – had been a bit more prickly, shifting about, kicking the turf, mouth working around his face like tightly stretched elastic. But Bisley was like that with everybody and either his gran didn't notice, or didn't care.

Damon and his gran ate the game pie from the butcher's in front of the tiny telly perched on a spindly table intended for pot plants. A neighbour had put the table out with the rubbish but his gran had retrieved it, given it a good scrub and, now, pride of place in the sitting room. Damon chewed slowly, hoping to ward off indigestion. His gran was getting on and wasn't too fussed about expiry dates. When he remembered, he'd go through her fridge and chuck out anything past its sell by. He'd started doing the tins in the cupboard too. On his last visit he'd found a can of custard five years out of date.

– I'm a lot more out of date than that, son. Better chuck me in the bin, too, she shrieked.

The news worked its way down from murders, motorway nightmares, suicide bids, a teen mum with multiple personalities and a middle-aged glazier leading a double life, to the sports. First the tennis – Wimbledon had just got under way – then cricket, cycling, finally the racing.

– Here's you, son.

Damon sawed up another mouthful of pie. It was gamey, no doubt about that. How gamey, was the question.

– Lovely race. Poetry in motion. And I'm ten pound up the day. Our dinner's paid for.

The carriage clock on the mantelpiece ticked loudly. The little metal balls which swung to and fro around its base seemed to make time slow down, run backwards.

There wasn't much of a mid-week crowd. A few strollers out enjoying the still light summer evening. Damon peered into

The Great Wall, a deep, low-ceilinged building, dim as an ocean shelf. Staring hard at the menu taped to the window, without seeing the long list of dishes which the kitchen could throw together in a matter of minutes, he felt the same as before a race – empty and too full. And his gran's pie wasn't to blame. He could have phoned, avoided the uncertainty but then it would have become a date, a commitment. Phoning hadn't been an option but this wasn't the right way either. He'd already eaten. And couldn't eat again.

The interior had been done up. Black and red lacquer. Rich and dark and classy. The waitress who showed him to a table wore a slinky Cheongsam. No more floppy trousers and tacky striped smocks. And no sign of Han. Maybe he'd taken the night off. To look around town for him? Or avoid him. Odds on avoiding him. Which made sitting in Han's restaurant, not even able to eat, a very stupid move.

A warm hard pressed Damon's shoulder.

– You want to order?

– I've eaten already. At my gran's. And suffering for it.

Han's half-shut eyes flickered. He took a deep draw on his cigarette and shot a plume of smoke between them.

– So you didn't come for the food.

– Did I ever? You've put on weight.

– You haven't.

– Well, no, sweetie. Some of us have to be discliplined, don't we?

The beginnings of a beer gut strained Han's tight white shirt. A stringy little goatee ran round his soft chin.

– You're working. I should have phoned.

– You're here now.

– Had a winner today. Totally out of the blue.

– I know.

– You were there? Why didn't you let me know?

– I'm letting you know now.

– If I hadn't come looking for you…

– But you did.

– And here I am. So how's business?

– So, so. More competition these days. Lots of new places. Thai, Vietnamese, Korean. People want new tastes. Something different on the tongue.

– Mm. Put anything on the Lord?

– Didn't like the look of him.

– Me neither.

Han called the waitress and asked her to bring over a couple of beers.

– Or are you on diet coke?

– Fuck you.

Han grinned, sat down and pushed back his hair which now had a pure white streak through it, coarse and glittering like salt. He swept away the place settings with his arm. Though Han had changed the décor, the chopsticks, glassware, table linen and the music – which now sounded more like Chinese parlour jazz than monks in temples – the napkins were still folded in the shape of lotus flowers.

– Maybe you should try a new shape for the napkins, said Damon. Fleur-de-lys. You could do that with a napkin.

– Why would I want to?

– Dunno. For luck.

– I didn't put money on your horse.

– Bloody well should have.

When the beer was finished, Han told the waitress he'd be back at closing time. Damon followed him through the smoky, spicy kitchen and up the back stairs. In the small flat above the restaurant, all the rooms faced the street. It was beginning to get dark but Han left the lights off. Even in the gloom, Damon could see the place was a tip.

– So you're not seeing anybody?

– Who said?

– Look at this place, man. When you've got downstairs so nice.

– Maybe, said Han, I just don't entertain at home.

They sat by the window in sagging armchairs. In the flats across the road, lights were on, curtains and windows were open. The heat was rare for this part of the world and folk were airing their houses, their lives.

– Your hands are rough, said Han.

– And you're getting fat.

Damon heard the kids across the street squabbling, a loud TV drama cranking up the aggro, somebody crashing a vacuum cleaner around, drunks below the window bellowing a staggered duet, Han's fast breath in his ear and a disembodied voice in the room: *Come on Illusions, come on The Lord!* In the half dark, on the floor of Han's bedraggled living room a strung-out seamless hybrid, half man, half horse, raced towards the post.

Timothy

LOVES HIMSELF. CAN'T get him away from a mirror. In the studio he goes right down the front so nobody blocks his view. Always gets a big solo in the shows too but that's because there's only him and flat-foot Torquil to choose between. We're lucky if we're seen on stage at all because there's tons of us. The boys have a whole changing-room to themselves while ours is like a total crush. When he was wee his mum made him wear tights under his shorts so he wouldn't catch cold and didn't cut his hair until he was like eight and let him play with her make-up and gave him a dressing-up box full of her old skirts and high heels and wouldn't let him play football in case he hurt himself or got bullied and didn't think there was anything weird about him wanting to watch *Riverdance* and *Billy Elliot* like a hundred times or go out guising dressed as The Lilac Fairy. But he can lift up all the girls even Gemma. And he can do higher jetés than anybody.

A Beautiful Restoration

BEFORE THE NAZIS and the Communists, pani Anna will say, this place was a palace.

My boss is not really talking to me, she's just thinking aloud. Though the exterior of the hotel is soot black, it is still beautiful. But the interior has suffered and, for pani Anna, restoration has become something of an obsession. She has spent many thousand zlotys on it. The cost of the wallpaper alone would have been enough for me to buy a small apartment. Guests like the result, especially foreigners. If I meet them in the corridor as they're going out to find breakfast and I'm off home to sleep after a night shift, they smile and say good morning. In the place I was before, which hasn't changed at all since independence, I was only ever greeted by grunts and groans.

I like the night. I can get on with my work without too many interruptions and when I'm done there's no need to pretend to be busy. Mostly it's ironing, folding and stacking linen and filling up the trolley with soap, bottled water, shower gel and shampoo, toilet rolls and bin bags. And things going wrong – a light bulb exploding, the batteries of a TV remote running down, a toilet becoming blocked. On night shift I don't like sorting toilets while the guests, in their night clothes, stand over me and get in the way, or sprawl on the beds and behave as if I'm not there.

Worse can happen. There's illness – for some reason guests need a doctor much more often at night than during the day when it's a lot easier to get hold of one. During the small hours I've witnessed one birth and two deaths: one death simply from drink, the other from drink and sex and heart failure combined. Drink causes a lot of trouble and mess, spilled or broken bottles, blood and vomit on the carpet, the bed, the wallpaper. Mess and fights. I deal with the mess but for fights I call Dmitri, the night porter. He's big and strong and doesn't waste time, just barges in. If the door is bolted on the inside, Dmitri presses his bony forehead against the door and says:

– You have one minute, starting from now, before I break in.

So far, Dmitri's threat has always worked, which is just as well. Pani Anna wouldn't be too happy about a broken door. In fact, I think Dmitri would be more likely to lose his job over a broken door than a smashed nose.

And visitors: I see the girls in their narrow heels and split skirts flitting down the corridors like moths. I see them sneaked into the lifts and, later, hustled down the back stairs and out into the night. I see the room the next morning. The girls are better fed these days and probably own prettier underwear now that there's more than black market goods to choose from. Pani Anna knows this kind of things goes on but as long as guests and visitors are discreet, it meant nothing to her. For Housekeeping it means extra work – more linen and towels to be changed, more airing of rooms and scrubbing stains off the new soft carpets.

Pani Anna cares a lot about carpets, wallpaper, about furnishings, and dreams of restoring downstairs to exactly how it was before the Nazis and the Communists: marble columns, gleaming wood panelling, flashing chandeliers and heavy damask drapes. The work is a long way from finished and she worries constantly about running out of money. The new government has given her some financial help – the hotel is an important historic building – but not enough.

– Not nearly enough, says pani Anna, With the costs of material and labour rising every day. And just look at the news: Deficit may sink zloty. Where will we all be then?

The zloty is not a ship. How can it sink, or float? All I know is that I need every shift and the extra money from washing clothes to make ends meet.

Pani Anna has a friend in Germany, a man who makes money from money. He has promised – for what reason she hasn't said though Dmitri and I have our ideas – not to let her plans for a beautiful restoration collapse into tragedy or farce. But often, after a phone call, pani Anna is angry or gloomy, or both. She sits at reception, rests her pale round elbows on the newly varnished horseshoe desk and drinks scotch soda. She won't touch Polish vodka and don't even mention Russian! A good-looking woman, though the whisky and the worry are making her grey and puffy around the eyes. She should go out more, sit in the sun. Summer will not last forever.

Of course the hotel has always had more interesting guests than drunken, whoring businessmen. Its fame comes not only from its frozen music, as pani Anna calls the architecture of the building. These are not her own words; they belong to somebody famous, I don't know who. In the past, the hotel was host to many famous people. It was here that in the year I was born, an International Congress was held. Writers and artists, film stars and philosophers gathered in this very building to discuss what to do about our poor, devastated country. People say pan Picasso first drew his famous fat dove of peace here, in this very building.

At that time, the interior was in a very bad condition, smashed windows and furniture, charred walls. There was a paper shortage too – well, there was a shortage of almost everything. People say that pan Picasso first drew the dove on his bedroom wall. The register from the congress disappeared – some say it was confiscated by the secret police, others that it went up in flames but anyway it's gone, so nobody knows who slept where. Maybe the story of the dove on the wall is just a legend. A place like this has many legends, one on top of the other.

Now, after a long absence, we have international visitors again, for the festival. During the day, music spills from the bedrooms, clear and sparkling as mineral water. From room seventy-seven I've been hearing the most heavenly singing. The voice belongs to a young Italian who even after being up very late – I know how late! – will stop in the corridor, sweep back his hair, put a hand on his heart and bow. This is an act: I know he is practising and I am a substitute for his audience but still I blush and simper and scurry off to my housekeeping room as if I'm very busy, as if I've just remembered some urgent task. Really, I'm embarrassed and ashamed of my dry, colourless hair, my cheap shoes.

Dmitri says he's a gay. He says this because the singer – whose name, I think, should be Angelo but is Giuseppe – doesn't sing in his deep speaking voice but high as a woman.

– Sounds like a castrato, Dmitri says. And the costume! Have you seen his costume? High-heeled boots, frilly blouse. A gay. Crime against nature, he says, pleased with himself and his certainty.

God, everybody knows this country has seen real crimes against nature – and not just seen them. But I don't argue with him. On the night shift, I have no-one else to call on and sometimes I really need big, bison-headed Dmitri to help me out.

And yes, I have seen the singer's clothes. I have some of them with me at this moment; the shirt with the lace cuffs, the high boots with the silver buckles. He called me to his room, around one. He had changed out of his costume into jeans and a white T–shirt. His chin was blue with stubble and his arms were covered with thick, dark hair, like fur. He is not tall and his nose is too big to call his face perfect but what does perfect mean but a set of rules? He was tired and a little tipsy – not drunk, not like the stringless puppets you can see on every street corner – but bright-eyed, lit up. His bedside table was strewn with bouquets of flowers, still in their cellophane.

– Please, one moment, I said, and rushed out of the room.

All I had in my supplies cupboard was an ugly ceramic jug, not nearly big enough and with a crazy slogan on the side: *The Flowering State.* That just would not do. I phoned reception.

– Bring me vases, Dmitri. Blue ones. Two or three.

– Blue ones are only for reception.

– Blue vases, Dmitri. Please. And hurry.

Dmitri never does anything quickly. I went out into the corridor and paced about in front of the lift. I should have fetched the vases myself. The flowers would be in water already, the singer would be bending his head, hair falling into his eyes, burying his face in the blooms, turning his big nose from side to side, breathing in the perfume...

Dmitri's head appeared in the glass window of the lift. The door creaked open and he stepped out, a blue glass vase wedged in the crook of each arm, his big, pocked face pressed between them. Good vases he'd brought me, with heavy, swirly bases. Hard to knock over.

– Who puts flowers in water at this time of night?

– The Italian, I said. Thanks.

Dmitri noisily sucked air through his crowded teeth and clumped back into the lift.

By the time I reached the singer's door I was out of breath and, I expect, red in the face. It's still so hot, even at night, though the leaves on the trees have turned gold and begun to fall. I knocked on the door with my elbow. When Giuseppe opened it and saw me standing there, half-hidden by blue glass, he gave me such a smile that I thought I would drop the vases and break them as well as my toes but then... then he took my face in his cool hands and – I still don't quite believe it – kissed me on both cheeks and ushered me into his room.

Giuseppe, the angel Giuseppe filled the vases with water and asked me to help him arrange the flowers, one vase each. This is not normally part of my duties but who would refuse such a sweet-smelling task? It was more of an honour than a chore to sit at the oval, glass-topped table, selecting stems from the bouquets spread in front of me. Roses, lilies, chrysanthemums; the perfume rising from the table, curling around us, drifting into our nostrils, mouths, our hair. The angel Giuseppe didn't squeeze the stems the way Dmitri does when pani Anna asks him to arrange displays for reception. He balanced them on an open palm and used his fingertips to guide them into position. Stems matter. Stems are like arteries. I've told Dmitri this but he continues to clamp them in his big fist. So, I suppose, he doesn't look like a gay.

While we were arranging the flowers the angel Giuseppe spoke to me, in Italian. I know the sound of the language because, on night shift, I sometimes listen to opera on the radio. It makes a change from the American pop music people can't get enough of these days. I couldn't understand a word but I could hear the angel's voice squeaking and grating, his throat hurting.

– Too much singing, he said, pointing to his open mouth.

His lips were red from wine, teeth white: no gaps, no twisted stumps. His tongue, I could see his tongue, pink and curling. My ears burned; I was blushing again. I slipped the last few stems into the vase and stood up.

– Excuse me, something else you want?

My English is horrible but Italian for me is no more than a wish, a dream.

– Yes, yes, I forget...

Praising my flower arrangement over his own, he went through to the bathroom and returned with his boots and shirt.

– Please, can you clean for tomorrow?

– Yes, yes, no problem. Thank you, please, I said, nodding
and back out of the room like a grovelling servant in a bad film.

Earlier tonight, before the singer distracted me, I was ironing
pillowcases and looking up from those endless bleached squares
at the old, stained wallpaper which was jumping with red and
green dots after all that white. I was thinking about pan Picasso
and his fat dove, and wondering how many times the walls
had been papered since the year of my birth.

Now, in my housekeeper's room, the door is locked and I'm
alone with my magazines, my kettle and tea bags, the stacks of
ironed linen and towels. The linen is of course white, the towels
too. There are plenty of good enough red (now pink) ones from
before independence but pani Anna won't have them used unless
a guest disgraces him – or herself. (I don't think many guests
understand pani Anna's towel code.) Nearly always it's a man
who slips up, or a man and woman together but I try to be
open-minded, not to discriminate. There has been – and sadly
still is, too much discrimination. Already, in the newly restored
old town, over fresh, cheerful paint in colours we haven't seen
for decades, the spray can and stencil graffiti are again making
their ugly, hateful marks. After living with grey crumbling
buildings for so long, with broken windows, broken promises
and captive spirits, could we not for a short while enjoy the
cheeriness of fresh paint, the calm sheen of unsmashed glass?
It's a small improvement, not important, I know, but this
country has seen so much destruction. Too much, too many
lives crushed by one set of rules or another, this country which
has the shape of a jellyfish – out and in, here and there, stretch
and squeeze – a strong, stubborn jellyfish all the same, one
which refuses to die no matter how many times it's stamped
on. But what must it be like to live in a country with fixed,
definite outlines, borders which haven't strayed for centuries,
like Italy, say, a shapely high-heeled boot dipping its toe in the

Mediterranean?

Carefully I put down the angel Giuseppe's boots so as not to mark the leather which is soft and supple and smells like money. It does, it really does smell like banknotes – or else banknotes smell like good Italian leather. I pick up the shirt; such fine cotton, it's almost transparent, weighs nothing. I press it to my face and breathe in sweat and cologne; olives, sun, salt. I breathe in and in until my head spins and I have to sit down on the old battered chair in which I've passed many quiet night hours.

Most of the guests will be asleep. Dmitri will be watching late night TV at reception, hoping that none of the stragglers falling in from the casinos will want room service – vodka, beer, champagne, cheese, ham, caviar. The angel Giuseppe will be lying on his big bed, naked I expect, naked I'm sure in this heat, on his back or his side, his head resting on the pillowslip I ironed last night. How differently I'd have ironed the linen had I thought about that: I'd have pressed it smooth with the flat of my hand, the weight of my body.

It's quiet now, except for the generator from which there is no escape. Even if I doze off in my chair I can hear its eternal grumble. No silence here, even in sleep. I fill the sink. The water mustn't be too hot, only warm, and the soap mild. I test the temperature with my elbow. Too hot. I leave it to cool down. In time it will reach the ideal temperature – blood heat. The room, too, is hot, airless, a tatty box. I toss my cardigan on the chair. No need to be tidy. Nobody ever comes here. Soon I'll wash the shirt, polish the boots...

Taking off my cardigan wasn't enough; it felt like another half-measure, another compromise and now that all my clothes are on the chair it's easy to pull the shirt over my head, slip my rough, blunt fingers through the lace cuffs and let the fine white cotton slide down and cover my nakedness, cover but not obscure the neglected architecture of my body, as pani

Anna might say. The boots stand beneath my ironing board, a little dusty, of course, you can't have restoration without dust... the boots also. Only a little too big. Not heavy at all and cool against my hot legs. I unpin my hair, let it fall around my shoulders. It doesn't exactly swing when I turn my head, it doesn't fall over my face like a curtain when I place a hand on my heart and bow. No sound comes when I open my mouth but here, in my ugly little room, dressed in the angel Giuseppe's shirt and boots, it occurs to me that this could once have been a bedroom. Anybody might have slept in it, even pan Picasso.

With the spatula I use to shift stubborn clots of mud from the shower cubicles, I pick loose a corner of wallpaper and begin to scrape. The strip peels off quite easily at first, right down to the yellow plaster. Then it becomes stubborn and clings to the wall. In the top corner of the plaster, a faint curving line swings between two raw edges of paper. I go back to where I started from and loosen the next strip. It, too, curls away. The curving line continues across the newly-bared patch of wall. Above it, I can now see a small black dot, like an eye. I keep scraping. With the angel's voice in my head, the memory of his mouth on my cheek, I too become part of a beautiful restoration.

The Shape of her Head

– GOING SOMEWHERE SPECIAL today?

– Not unless a solicitor's office qualifies. I do wish you people wouldn't keep asking that question.

– Sorry.

– It's demoralising. Makes people think they haven't got a life.

– Temperature OK for you?

– It's fine.

– This is a really good new product. Specially formulated for relaxation as well as conditioning.

– Let's hope it works. I've been up to high doh this week with one thing and another and this afternoon's meeting will no doubt hike my blood pressure up into the danger zone.

– Well just you sit back and make the most of a bit of pampering while you can.

– Don't worry. I like to get what I pay for.

Harriet's thin, pencilled eyebrows zigzag above pressed shut eyes, a sharp nose, a mouth like a block of mauve in a colour chart, a strong, square jaw. Beneath Kerry's gently kneading fingers, Harriet's hair stands up in steel-grey oily peaks.

In a gentle circling motion, Kerry continues to massage hot oil infused with essence of lavender and ylang ylang into her client's scalp, humming along to the new Kylie single crackling away muddily on the radio. Craig should really fork out for a decent sound system, seeing as the salon staff have to listen to it all day long. Outside, crowds of high school kids on their lunch break straggle past the big windows, chomping on sandwiches and slabs of pizza, swigging down fizzy drinks. Kerry's eyes pick out a couple of familiar faces. Chris and Tommy. Chris looks just the same; sandy hair flopping into his eyes, weedy beneath a baggy sweatshirt. Tommy's grown a bit and sprouted a fuzzy beard with more red in it than his hair. A couple of years ago she'd have been out the door of wherever she was, tailing them, hoping Tommy would turn round and notice her. A couple of years ago she'd hung out after school on the steps of the paved courtyard up by the uni, which the skateboarders and winos had made their own. A couple of years ago, she'd sat for hours in all weathers, cold stone chilling her arse, hoping an opportunity to communicate with Tommy would come up. It never quite did.

– Will you take a look at that lot, says Harriet, pointing a long mauve nail in the direction of the window. A disgrace to their uniforms, chomping away in public like that. And roaming around can't be good for the digestion. I don't see why the authorities can't insist on school lunches. At least that way young people would be assured of some nutritional value. You really can't trust them to eat sensibly when there's all that carryout rubbish around. And sitting at a table eating with friends is so much more civilised than munching on the pavement.

Kerry remembers being taught that it was rude to point. And remembers the mad battle of the dinner hall, the kickings, the kneeings and the elbowings, the clatter of crockery, the screech of stainless steel, the suffocating smell of bodies and food, the rush to get your meal down before the teachers hustled you out to make room for the next sitting.

– I never liked school dinners.

– Nobody likes school dinners. You aren't meant to like them.
But if you're hungry you eat them. And they do you good.

– You doing OK, there?

– I'll let you know if I'm not.

The hot oil head massage is a new treatment Craig introduced
last month, offering a reduced introductory rate and sweet-
talking the regulars into giving it a go. So far, it's been very
popular, not just with women, men have taken to it as well.
Craig's live-in partner Jeff, even though he's a master stylist
and usually doesn't lift a finger unless it involves scissors or a
blow dryer, has volunteered once or twice to stand in for Kerry.
The girls had a good laugh about that but Craig was none too
pleased.

Kerry has received no training in head massage – and so far
very little in hairdressing – but as she's been booked solid for
the past few weeks, she's had plenty practice and has got the
hang of keeping her fingers moving in a steady, soothing rhythm:
not too fast, not too slow, not too hard, not too soft. There
hasn't been much more in her pay cheque but the tips have
been better than when she was on shampooing and Craig says
that if she's serious about her career she should take every
opportunity to extend her skills. And Craig's the boss.

It's still an hour until her break. Under the general roar of
blowdriers, Kerry can hear her stomach gurgling. Craig likes
the staff to stagger their lunches and stay on the premises, which
means eating a sandwich on your own in a smoky, windowless,
basement room. Sometimes when she's in the groove, the noise
of the salon fades away and she slips into a daydream about
being with Scott on a holiday in the sun. Sometimes her eyes
get heavy and she nearly drops off while she's standing over a
customer. She talks to keep herself awake.

– Looks nice out.

– It's cold.

– Bright at least.

– Strong sunlight gives me a headache.

– That's a shame. I used to get headaches when I was wee. My gran used to massage my temples to take away the pain. Ahead of her time, she was.

– A headache's the least of my worries. I thought chucking out my husband would be a simpler business than it's turning out to be.

– Oh. Sorry.

– Sorry I've chucked my husband out or sorry it's proving to be a problem?

Kerry eases her fingers out from the centre of Harriet's forehead towards the temples and wishes she'd kept her mouth shut. But it's not always easy. When a customer tells you something, you can't just grunt or go off to fetch something you don't really need, even if it's the safest thing to do. Craig says it's rude not to respond to what a customer's been saying and if there's one thing he comes down hard on staff for it's being rude to customers. He has a spiel he trots out to all his new recruits. It goes something like:

Do you know what I've had to put up with over the years to make this place a success? I've sold my soul. Flattered and lied, day in, day out. Colour, style, that stuff's a dawdle. Opinions are the killer. You've got to have an opinion about their children, spouses, significant others, about politics and religion and sex and the state of the world and it's got to correspond with each and every one of their opinions. They don't come here for a debate on anti-terrorist laws, teenage pregnancies or gay marriages. They come to be pampered and agreed with. And don't you forget it.

– Well, which?

– I just… I just meant sorry you're having a hard time of it.

– Oh, it's not so bad. I've been thinking about it for long

enough. Now I've finally got around to it, I wish I'd made the break years ago. I'll have to lie to my solicitor, though. Nothing dreadful. But I couldn't tell him the truth.

Harriet's ringed fingers dart around her lap like flashy birds.

– I couldn't really tell my husband the truth either.

– The truth.

Kerry knows she sounds like a moron but you don't go asking somebody why they chuck their husband out, though it's the obvious question on your mind. If a customer wants to spill the beans then you've no choice but to listen for as long as it takes. Or as long as what you're doing takes and a head massage takes a lot longer than a shampoo. Listening's not so bad but there always comes a point when a customer expects a response. That's the tricky bit. It's not always easy to find the right thing to say, so to be on the safe side, you say something stupid.

– I'll have to come up with some boring rubbish about the breakdown of communication.

– Right.

You repeat what the customer just said, or you say: Really? OK. Right. No! You're joking! I know what you mean. And after a while you start to feel like a moron. Some of the newer salons play the radio so loud it's impossible to have a conversation. This would solve the problem but Craig says loud music puts off the silver pound and he doesn't want to lose his older clientele because they're more loyal. They like what they know and come back year after year if you give them what they know. The young, Craig says, are fickle. They move on and move away. Craig's an old fart.

– The truth. Yes. The truth is I don't like the shape of his head.

– Your solicitor's head?

– No, no – I couldn't care less about the shape of my solicitor's head. My husband's head. I don't like the shape of my husband's head.

– That's a new one.

Kerry allows herself a small, guarded smile.

– Actually, it's not new at all. Rather old, in fact. Almost two hundred years old. People used to think that you could tell all sorts of things about a person from the shape of the head. Intelligence, generosity, an aptitude for poetry or numbers, a strong sex drive, a predisposition to violence, even good parenting skills. Phrenology, it was called. They did just what you do, the phrenologists, applied their fingertips to the head in question and interpreted personality from bumps on the skull. If your head was bigger in a certain area it meant you had more of whatever attribute was located there. They consulted head maps to see what the ideal size of each part was. I went to an interesting lecture on the subject. With plaster casts of the heads of famous statesmen, scientists, artists, murderers and so on. The whole thing was discredited for a number of reasons, but I'm not convinced the phrenologists were so way off beam. Anyway, after that lecture, I started looking at the shape of people's heads and every time I looked at my husband's, I thought: That's not a reliable head, not well-balanced. It juts out at the front as if it's ready to jab at whatever it comes up against. A woodpecker sort of head. That's not the head of a man I want to be married to. Of course, I can't tell that to my solicitor.

– No.

– He'd think I was barking. It is the ultimate reason, though. It is the truth. Silly as it may sound. There's nothing really wrong with my husband, nothing you could put your finger on. But nothing really right either. Do you have a boyfriend?

– Yes. Scott. We've been going out for nearly nine months. He's in catering.

– Good for him. Always work in that field. People need to eat. But you should check out the shape of his head. Look out for negative tendencies.

– We're saving up for a deposit on a flat.

– I wouldn't rush into shacking up. Keep your independence as long as you can. If you're interested in having children, the good parenting part of the head is supposed to be up from the nape of the neck. Above libido.

– Have you been married long?

– Too long. Nothing's meant to last forever. All that *Till Death Us Do Part* – hooey, if you ask me.

– It's a big step, all the same. Splitting up.

– Oh I don't know. I think people are too namby-pamby sometimes. Creeping along, scared to put a foot wrong. Where does that get you? My daughter's forever telling me I should have thought it over longer, postponed making a decision. But I say: She who hesitates is lost.

– How many children do you have?

– Just the one, thankfully. And she's more or less off my hands now. I can't understand the fuss she's made about the split. It's not as if she's going to lose out. Her education's been taken care of and she'll have two abodes to bring her dirty washing home to.

– Children can take these things quite bad.

– Well they shouldn't. I can understand if there's a lot of unpleasantness, or if they find themselves pawns in some ghastly acrimonious game. But if everything is kept civil and above board, I really can't see a problem.

Kerry recognises most of the kids on the street from school. She didn't like school. Got out at the first opportunity. For a year she's shampooed hair and swept it up off the floor, made tea and coffee, fetched magazines and ashtrays, answered the phone. In the park across the road, the daffodils have just come out, hundreds of them. Three girls are sprawled on a bench, knee deep in daffodils, heads tilted back to catch the sun on their faces. Chris and Tommy pass the window again, in the opposite direction. This time they have a girl squeezed between them. Is it Gina? Gina and Kerry had been in Biology and

German together. If it is her, she's got a diabolical new hair colour. Kerry feels a pang but just a small, impersonal pang. Nothing important. Since she's been working, she doesn't see her old school friends much. Too busy studying. Exams and college applications. No time to meet.

Not that she's bothered. On payday she goes clubbing with a couple of the younger stylists. It's a laugh and they get into places she wouldn't get into on her own. And she's got Scott. He's OK. Sound. Her mum likes him. Better than Kerry does. Her dad's not met Scott yet but that's because he's now living at the other end of the country and Kerry hasn't seen him since she left school. He's invited her down any time she wants but she's not ready to meet her dad's new family yet. Not sure she ever will be.

– Nearly done. I'm going to apply a bit more pressure now. Let me know if it's uncomfortable.

With all her strength Kerry presses down on Harriet's warm, oily scalp, pushing the skin around, feeling it stretch and slide over skullbone. During the last year, Kerry's fingertips have worked their way over hundreds of heads: dry heads, flaky heads, scaly heads, greasy heads, heads covered in crispy hair, curly hair, thick hair, thin, silky, coarse hair, brittle, limp, flyaway hair, no hair at all; heads with lumps and bumps, ridges, scabs and scars; heads like melons, turnips, rugby balls, coconuts. Harriet's head is round and ridged like a small pumpkin. Kerry imagines having fingers of steel, fingers which could drill straight through bone to soft, pulpy, stupid brains.

Giselle

GISELLE SNIFFS AT the mention of flamenco: it's too hot and bothered for her taste, too extravagant, too *Latin*. Tap might be frivolous but flamenco – she sets her chin against late nights, loose morals and questionable men in tight trousers and approaches a shelving unit stacked with salmon pink *pointes*.

For each bright-eyed girl fidgeting on the lilac banquette of the dancewear shop she has tyrannised for thirty years, Giselle deliberately plucks out a whole shoe size smaller than requested. As the girls crush their toes against the blocks and wince as they rise into first and then second position, Giselle insists that she has fitted them all correctly.

– They should be on the very edge of excruciating. You have to suffer for art, she says, without a shred of pity.

Pornographers at Lunch

AT A TABLE on the balcony of a legendary Barcelona restaurant just off the Ramblas, Xavier, Juan Carlos and Elisabeta sit amidst the remains of their lunch, a fish-shaped platter of mixed seafood and a second bottle of *cordoniu seco*. Elisabeta, squat and businesslike in a charcoal trouser suit, has just downed the last oyster and now fingers a pearl earring, pale and luminous against her dark, downy cheek. Across the table, Xavier blots traces of olive oil and melted butter from the corners of his full, soft mouth. A dove grey jacket and lemon shirt hang loosely from his shoulders. His broad face is as yet unsmiling but Elisabeta knows from the flickering puckers around his mouth that he is, gastronomically at least, satisfied. Next to Xavier, Juan Carlos, dark and sleek as a cormorant, attacks the last crispy morsels of clams in breadcrumbs. Elisabeta is not in the least concerned about Juan Carlos' satisfaction. He will take what he gets, do, eventually, as he is told.

It is late afternoon. Their table is next to the staircase, up and down which a couple of progressively weary waiters tread in seamless, overlapping loops. Elisabeta looks down through the elaborate modernista banister at other diners, heads still bowed over food. On the other side of the plate glass window those who have already eaten stroll, full-bellied in the still warm, still vital November sun. When Niño, their chubby, latte-skinned waiter stops to remove debris from the table, Xavier suggests cognac with coffee and of course Elisabeta agrees. There are few occasions on which she disagrees with Xavier and what he chooses to consume at a working lunch would never be one of them. But Juan Carlos, if he doesn't stop squawking about the need to find new markets, will soon find out just how disagreeable she can be.

When the plates have been cleared, Xavier sets his laptop on the table and boots up. Elisabeta puts on her glasses, black-rimmed, stylishly severe, and concentrates on the screen. The first image which comes up is the airbrushed face of a blonde, head thrown back, tongue curling between open lips.

– Sydney. Nice, isn't she, says Juan Carlos. Want to see more of her, don't you?

– Not really, no.

Xavier adjusts the image, scrolling down so that the whole of Sydney, naked and blatantly inviting, fills the screen.

– Not very subtle, says Elisabeta.

– She's not supposed to be subtle, says Juan Carlos. She's meant to do it for you and do it quickly. Does it for me.

– But the question is, says Xavier, does she do it for Elisabeta?

Elisabeta adjusts her glasses, rotates an earring between the pads of thumb and index finger, feels the pearl, warm and round and reassuring, graze the inside of her blunt-cut nails.

– She's too much in my face, says Elisabeta.

– You want her in a bikini? says Juan Carlos. With her legs crossed? Porn has to hit you in the balls. Or wherever.

– I don't want her at all, says Elisabeta. That's my point.

Xavier sighs mildly, glances at his watch. It is close to four. Lunch has been long and slow and delicious but they must return to the office in an hour, to meet clients.

– It's the details we need to think about, says Xavier. Are the details doing their job?

He clicks, zooms on to Sydney's face, eyes closed, mouth open in a crass parody of ecstasy.

– Too dry. The *details* need more moisture, says Elisabeta.

– Fuck, says Juan Carlos. You dykes are fussy.

– Aren't we.

Xavier readjusts the image, stopping again on full frontal.

– Elisabeta's right, he says. Back to the drawing board for Sydney.

Juan Carlos flaps about in his seat, jabs a dessert fork into the tablecloth

– Please, says Elisabeta. I'd like to be able to come back here.

– Do you have any idea how long I spent on that slut? says Juan Carlos.

– Clearly not long enough, says Xavier.

Xavier double clicks. Sydney disappears. The waiter returns, bearing a small tray containing three cognacs, three café solo and a small dish of cakes. He sets everything down then moves on to attend to the next table. Xavier picks up a miniature croissant, its horns dipped in dark chocolate. He turns it around and says, with all the seriousness of a young child:

– What about this, Elisabeta? Too much in your face?

Elisabeta plucks the pastry from his hand and pops it in her mouth.

– Mmm. Mmm, mmm!

– Maybe we should switch right over to gastroporn, says Juan Carlos. If dykes are anything to go by.

Elisabeta chomps on her croissant. Juan Carlos sloshes his cognac around.

At the next table, their waiter is struggling to comprehend the questions asked by a trio of tourist women who can neither understand the menu nor decide what they want from it.

– The trouble is, says Xavier, people don't know what they want until they see it.

– And we have to make sure that when they see it, that's how they react.

Elisabeta indicates one of the tourist women who is pointing at and requesting a dish of food which she sees being delivered to another table.

– Even, she adds, if what they're looking at is road-kill crow.

Xavier winces. Elisabeta finds his squeamishness endearing.

Xavier throws another image on to the screen; another woman, this time a brunette, in stimulus mode. This time the flesh is dressed with a garnish of chains and studded leather. Juan Carlos lights a cigarette, waves it around.

– So is Paloma more your style, then?

Elisabeta looks closely at the screen, taking in the contrast between black leather and tanned skin, the positioning of thighs and fingers, the tilt of the head, then rests her elbows on the table in the manner of someone about to instigate an arm wrestling contest.

– Well? says Juan Carlos.

– Tired.

– What d'you mean tired? This is hot. This stuff's always hot. You having trouble with your hormones?

Elisabeta helps herself to another cake, a roll of sponge dusted with icing sugar and stuffed with pureed figs. She lifts it to her mouth, bites it in half, surrenders herself to taste.

– Mmm! You should try one of these, Juan Carlos. These are *inspiring*.

– Why do I have to be at the mercy of a sugar junkie?

– Elisabeta doesn't always know best, says Xavier. But we always value her opinion.

– Might as well ask a monkey about ballet.

Xavier raises a finger to his lips. Juan Carlos stubs out his cigarette, tips another from the pack, lights up and blows more smoke across the table. Niño comes by with a fresh ashtray, catches sight of the leather-clad object of desire on the screen, opens his mouth, shuts it again.

– Hot, huh? says Juan Carlos? She's hot, right?

– Say what you like, Niño, says Elisabeta. My colleagues appreciate feedback. And I won't tell on you for looking.

– I'm a married man, señora.

– I know. I've met your wife. A lovely woman.

– Want to watch your old lady around that one, says Juan Carlos. One day she might come home and announce she's a lesbo.

Embarassment flushes the waiter's face.

– It's OK, says Elisabeta. Juan Carlos shouldn't drink *cordoniu* at lunchtime.

– Married men are allowed fantasies, too, Niño, Juan Carlos croons thickly. Give us your thoughts on Paloma. Please.

– You want me to be honest?

– Please, man, says Juan Carlos. We need some honesty around this table. No more bullshit. No more bulldyke shit.

Xavier smiles encouragement at Niño, who smooths down his long, still pristine apron. Elisabeta pops the remainder of a fig roll into her mouth, strokes her chin and chews slowly.

– Well, says Niño, the girl in the picture is blonde, tanned, skinny. I like a big woman, with red hair and white skin.

– Like your wife, says Elisabeta.

– Of course, says Niño.

– But what about the gear, man? Doesn't that stuff get you hot?

With the back of a baby-fat hand, the waiter wipes sweat from his forehead and dutifully continues to stare at Paloma.

– Coming up and down the stairs gets me hot, señor. And the kitchen, the kitchen gets me very hot. You want anything else here?

– No, says Xavier. Thank you.

– It's nothing, says Niño.

The waiter moves on swiftly to the table of tourist women

who are scouring their phrase book in search of some difficult questions of their own.

The restaurant is beginning to empty out. Downstairs, only a handful of people still eat and a few more linger over drinks and cigarettes. Waiters whip off tablecloths the way flamenco dancers snap their skirts. They ferry trays piled high with dirty dishes towards the kitchen. At the bar, the head waiter, frowning and chewing on a pencil stub, is trying to make sense of the evening reservations.

Elisabeta presses the fingertips of one hand into the cake crumbs on her plate, raises them to her mouth and, one by one, sucks. Though she has drunk much less than either Xavier or Juan Carlos she is not immune to the warm glow induced by good food and wine and the all too rare proximity of Xavier. There is, of course, the unavoidable adjunct of Juan Carlos but if she allows herself to admit it, his presence today might be said to add a little something.

– Next, she says.

Xavier clicks and a pedal bin appears on the screen, all chrome and steel with a decorative band of eliptical perforations round the rim. He zooms in on the foot pedal, activates the flashing green arrow, then minimises so the entire bin reappears on screen. Slowly the lid opens, revealing its inner rim from which hangs a silvery, virtual plastic bag. When the lid reaches its zenith, Xavier double clicks and it begins to descend slowly and conceal its virtual innards.

– The questions here are: Does the pedal work with the whole design? Does the lip drop at the optimum speed? Does the band of perforations enhance the rim?

– What's *her* name, then? says Elisabeta.

Juan Carlos spits a strand of black tobacco into his hand, blows his stinking smoke straight at Elisabeta's face. Though the smoke makes her eyes water, she refuses to blink.

– My question is, she says: Should the lid be flat? Wouldn't a rounded lid be more... enticing? Next.

– Where would we be without you, Elisabeta, says Xavier, clicking at the mouse.

Juan Carlos curses.

A bottle of shower gel appears on the screen, phallic in every possible respect, from the slippery bulbous cap to the ribbed column of the container. Elisabeta removes her glasses, wipes them with a silk rag, reinstates them on her snub nose.

– It's the meniscus you want to look at, says Xavier. The overall shape too, of course, and the relative proportion of bottle and cap. But the focus is the meniscus.

– Is that the actual size?

– My dear Elisabeta, Xavier smirks, I'll let you decide.

He zooms in on the detail in question, the place where the jade green gel ends in a dark swollen lip, where a sliver of translucence interrupts the green of the gel and the close but not quite matching green plastic of the cap. He reaches across the table, takes Elisabeta's small firm hand in his larger, softer one and, starting at the inner wrist, slowly strokes two fingers down the middle of her palm. When he reaches the forking paths of her spread fingers, he retracts his own in the lingering, wistful way oil disengages from glass.

Juan Carlos slugs down the dregs of his cognac. Xavier eases his slow, heavy body into a slack-kneed sprawl, lets his gaze drift around the restaurant and stop. He nods, he ruminates, he presses his lips together then gently releases them, like a child blowing bubbles. With the assistance of a large wall mirror behind the staircase, Elisabeta locates the object of Xavier's attention. At the neighbouring table of tourists, Niño is setting down a schooner of beer. The woman who ordered it rewards him with a dazzling smile. In the late afternoon light, the beer in the glass is yellow gold, effervescent, with a perfectly sexy head.

A Bewitched Embrace

OUR THROATS WERE dusty, our eyes screwed against the glare. We didn't speak. We were not speaking. We had not been speaking for seventy or eighty kilometres, since the last village, a pretty place with broad-leaved trees, flowering creepers and at least two roadside restaurants. You'd wanted to stop there, let the car cool down, stretch your legs. I was keen to push on, cover more ground. As I was driving, I got my way. The car clearly sided with you.

The lake, if it was one, was a poisonous green, the ravaged ground rust red. In every sense it was an unnatural landscape, a gouged-out hillside, a cavity, bare of any vegetation other than whatever mutant matter occupied the water. That was where the car failed to make yet another of the steep inclines I'd been pushing it over for the last hour and ground to a halt, accompanied by the choking stink of burnt rubber. It was the hottest time of the day and the sun bit into our necks and bare shoulders as we abandoned our smoking old banger and made for the village, for shade and – please, please – a cold drink.

We were the only customers in the only bar. The peeling

walls were adorned with a greasy saint and a dog-eared calendar featuring a team photo of Real Madrid. There was no sign of the proprietor. If we'd been speaking, you'd have reminded me of how nice the place we passed an hour before had looked, adding that there, even with a broken-down car, we night have enjoyed our stop instead of enduring it, that holidays were meant to be about enjoyment, not endurance. I know that would have been your line: we'd had the discussion/disagreement/argument before. They say, people say, people who do research into people – how they get on and don't get on, how they leap together like magnets or whirl apart like magnets – they say that your first argument is the one you go on having.

I was thinking about this when a woman who must have been in her sixties at least, emerged from a dark doorway behind the bar. Dyed black hair, too much kohl and lipstick, a tight teenager's skirt and high, scuffed heels, she blinked like a night creature hauled from the shadows and stunned by daylight. We asked for two limonadas. Without a word she opened our bottles, dropped our coins into the till and retired to her private darkness, leaving us to our tepid drinks, a rickety table and a squad of fat, buzzing flies. Outside, the dazed empty street simmered in the afternoon haze.

A dog wandered in, sniffed around our legs. You patted its matted head, let it lick your damp, salty knees. I pushed it away. I didn't kick it, I nudged it with my foot. It could as easily have been the other way round. Neither of us was a consistently committed animal lover. We didn't drool over fluffy puppies or cute kittens, just each other, though by then that too was becoming less consistently committed. As for the patting or pushing away, it could have been the other way round: it could have been me as Kind Princess and you as Hag. I didn't say this. We were still not talking. We were postponing talking for at least as long as the limonada lasted.

A wilderness lacking any picturesque connotations of the word, a valley gutted by open-cast mining with a one street, one bar village tacked on, wasn't the best place to break down. But enjoyment wasn't the point and, if we'd been talking, I'd have said we could have done a lot worse. On that road, we could have easily broken down with nothing in sight but flayed, mineral-rich earth. And soon we'd be gone. By the time we finished our drinks and walked back up the hill, the engine and the radiator would have cooled down. I'd turn on the ignition and our miraculous old car would once again revive. We'd continue on our way and, after a couple of hours, reach our destination in good enough time. As we roared up and down the switchback road, leaving the blasted landscape behind, we'd begin to look forward to the cabin we'd booked ahead months back.

Situated in pinewoods, our cabañas offer peace, seclusion and close encounters with nature. If that is not enough, a short walk brings you to our exclusive leisure complex: two pools, two restaurants, tennis courts, horse-riding, squash and mini-golf.

Amazing: I can still remember the blurb from the brochure. Well, maybe not so amazing. I'd quoted it so often over those winter months, chanted it like a mantra to get us through the dark and cold, the flues and blues, the electricity meter popping coins like a Royal Mint junkie.

Close encounters with nature made you giggle in that sexy, throaty way which made me want to get you there immediately. Indoors, especially in winter, you were modest and self-conscious in a way I found frustrating but outdoors turned you on, pinewoods in particular: the tang of conifers, sunlight slicing deep through green spears, the glisten of oozing, honey-coloured sap. Why else would I have agreed to such a long drive? Or you. Once we got going, you'd start to imagine the woods and we'd stop not speaking. Once we got going, the deadlock would be broken.

It was late afternoon by the time the breakdown lorry arrived, hoisted our dead car on to the trailer and delivered it, and us, to the garage where the only mechanic on our side of the sierra shook his head, rolled his eyes and demonstrated the magnitude of our problem like a fisherman extolling the one that got away. With the help of the phrase book and the man's frequent repetition of key words like *radiador, embrague, kaput* and *mañana*, we began to get some sense of what was wrong with the car. *Embrague* stumped me at first. I though our man with the corrugated forehead, steely halo of curls and oil black hands had said *embruje* which, according to my phrase book meant bewitched. The car had been bewitched by the poison lake, drugged by toxins, put to sleep by the heat? It needed dark and quiet and the love of a stranger to bring it back to life? When the mechanic pulled out the clutch disc as proof of our problem, it was as smooth as a CD, the bite entirely worn away.

We left the car keys at the garage and went in search of a room for the night. Even still, the *embruje/embrague* confusion hung around in my head. It was something to think about as we sulked and slogged down the hot road to the hot village while our secluded cabaña was waiting for us, nestling in cool, scented woods, out of reach. *Embruje*: bewitched. *Embrague*: clutch, grasp, embrace. A bewitched embrace. I'd have asked you if you fancied that, you and me fused together for an unimaginable length of time but as we were only communicating via clipped questions and grunted replies, I didn't.

Though siesta time was over, the village hadn't exactly brushed the sleep from its eyes, opened its doors and stepped out to greet the world on its only street. Still, we had an address. Above an open door, daubed on the wall: 22.

– My favourite number, I said. Like the two of us curled up for sleep.

Your response was noncommittal. In a doorway, a girl in a flouncy red and white dress squatted on the steps like a crushed Christmas cracker. With a stick, she poked at a beetle floundering on its back, unable to right itself. I asked about the room. You said something complimentary and insincere about the little tyrant's dress. Then you tried to persuade her to turn the poor thing over. You were definitely Kind Princess that day, patting a mangy dog and worrying about a beetle. Slowly, the girl looked us up and down. Eyes round and deep as straws, she sucked in our cropped hair, sweat-soaked vests, our bare legs. When she'd drunk us in down to our hiking boots, she patted the red bow in her hair and ran off to fetch her mother.

Our situation was so predictable, the premise for any number of movie plots. Car breaks down. Travellers stranded in strange place. Strange people. Strange goings on. The scenario as old as the hills. Chiller or heartwarming comedy. In the chiller, the travellers inevitably become prey to some inbred, prejudiced weirdos. In the comedy, after being treated as outcasts, they win through, transforming some inbred prejudiced weirdos into warm-hearted human beings. There was a movie we watched one time about a bunch of New York drag queens who set off for California and, en route, solved the social problems of some mid-west town. My favourite lines were spoken by a maltreated but finally empowered wife to the leading queen: *Soon as ah set eyes on you ah knowed you weren't no gel. A gel ain't got no Aidam's Aipple.* Something like that. Don't quote me.

Had we been getting on we might have taken up the challenge of trying to transform our avaricious landlady and her dour, overdressed daughter but this wasn't a movie and a plot line to push things on a bit, to drag us out of our own impasse, didn't materialise. Not did the *ventilador* we were promised to cool the air in our sweltering, overpriced boxroom. We'd thought about bringing the tent along in case something like this happened but where would we have pitched it? By the poison lake in the middle of the quarry?

We almost cancelled the holiday. We should have. I can see that now but hindsight's a fat lot of use and I can't even say you pushed for us to go because you didn't. I pushed for us to go and I pushed the damn car over one hill too many. I always was pushy. Which you liked, at first. I wanted to get there, to arrive, to reach the woods where you'd rub pine needles against your skin until they shot out their green scent, throw water in my face and catch droplets on your tongue as they splashed off me. I wanted to get there. Whoever said that the travelling and not the destination is all, is a fool.

We almost cancelled because, unlike many defunct industrial sites, the vast open-cast mine up the road would not be recycled as a museum. Unemployed miners would not be retrained as tour guides. Not long after we booked our holiday and immediately before the mine closed down, its reputation as a danger to public health greatly outweighed share values. Toxic waste broke its bins and flooded into the river, killing everything in it, in the fields fed by it and the wildlife sanctuary through which it flowed to the sea. The disaster made the international press. Worried, you brought me the newspaper article and the map. The map was bigger than the kitchen table and drooped over the edge like the crisply pressed tablecloth we never wanted and never had. Between your thumb and index finger lay the black spot and the beauty spot.

– They're close on the map, I said. But think of the scale.

– I am. This is a big-scale disaster. It must be.

– Maybe there was nothing else to put in the papers today. Maybe the editor's got a bee in his bonnet about toxic waste. Maybe it's World Ecology Week.

Like I said, I wanted to get there.

– It's the only piece about ecology.

– Maybe there's a series: one a day for a week. A month. A year. A worldwide survey. Maybe we'll find we've a toxic waste problem on our own doorstep.

Maybe: lifebelt for a drowning woman.

– I'm going to call the Foreign Office, you said. Travel Help Desk.

Why do I remember that entire conversation when I can't

remember what we said the last time we met? As it was, it was I who phoned the Travel Desk, to settle it, put your mind at rest. I looked up the number in your address book and found it under H for *Holiday*. And no, I wasn't sidetracked into combing the pages for unfamiliar names or enigmatic entries. The brisk, tight-lipped chap on the other end of the phone issued the official statement:

– We have no information on the area in question.

– Any advice, then?

– We have no information on the area.

We got to know that hot room very well, too well, the black constellations of dead mosquitoes on the flaky walls, the convoy of ants on the floor commandeering our crumbs of dry bread and sour, oily cheese. We also got to know each other too well, in the way cellmates or people confined in a small hospital ward get to know each other; obliged to share every breath, blink, sigh, cough, sniff, chew, swallow, scratch, rumble, belch, fart, snort, snore. After such relentless intimacy, desire hid beneath the beds.

Endurance was not the point of a holiday but endurance was our only option while the *embrague* was being replaced and the part for the *radiador* delivered from the other end of the country, apparently by donkey. Though we were lucky to have a room between us, separate rooms might have saved us. The landlady's preference for loud TV quiz shows didn't help, nor did her daughter's habit of skulking around outside our door, eye or ear to the keyhole – when did that child sleep? But the place and the people are blameless and irrelevant. The village shrank to the room. The room shrank to our bodies, on separate beds.

The heat was an enemy. If it had been cool, or better still, cold, at least we might have cuddled up for the sake of warmth. Instead, we sizzled and spat night after night, cooking in our own juices, the proximity of our bodies bearing no relation to closeness. Those slow hot hours, every day a replay of the one before – I have difficulty distinguishing them now. Other than the pre-breakfast trail to the garage, to hear yet another sincere apology from the mechanic, there was nothing to do but eat, drink, read, doze and blister with discontent. By the time the car was repaired, our money was done, our *cabaña* had been rented to a couple of cyclists and we were a lot further apart than just not speaking. I blame the lake.

Eclipse

OUTSIDE THE FRONT door with the home-made pinhole and a sheet of paper to catch the image of the about-to-be-obscured sun. Back to the blinding orb to protect the eyes as instructed. Above the rooftops the sky like tarnished brass. Birds and traffic quelled. A tiny bright dot on my sheet of paper. So far, so dull.

The neighbour, who's lived next door for years, appears on the other side of our mutual fence. We've never spoken. Now and again, I've heard him through the walls cursing something, somebody. He'll have heard the same from my side. It's what you hear of neighbours.

– Sorry to bother you, he says, his voice muted but clear in the unnatural hush. Have you had any trouble with your slabs? That cable TV lot cracked a couple of my slabs. Said they'd replace them but it's been weeks now.

– I didn't get cable, I said.

–Me neither. It's the laddies upstairs. Their ma wanted it put in for them. Fine with me but it's the slabs. Just thought

I'd ask. In case you'd had the same trouble.

The neighbour vaults the waist-high fence which surrounds his slabbed-over pocket of ground, goes back inside. I look at my own patch of dandelion-infested grass and, in the border, the clump of spindly flowers I've managed to grow from seed – anemones, cornflowers, love-in-a-mist. I was going for a blue theme. I don't have any slabs.

Through my living room window I can hear the TV countdown to what, in some places, is expected to be total eclipse. I try the pinhole business again. Maybe there's a minuscule dark ant eating into the firefly on my page, maybe not. It's no good, the pinhole. No drama at all. I go inside and catch Patrick Moore weeping – with joy at having survived long enough to witness this momentous occasion or disappointment that it didn't live up to expectations.

Months later, my neighbour and I still haven't met again since the eclipse. When we meet, if we do, we can talk about his dazzling new slabs. It will be years before they achieve a similar grime-grey drabness to those around them, years before I forget the eclipse.

The Absence of Light

– DO I LOOK like an Eskimo?

Gloria cracked open a can of Carlsberg. It was eleven in the morning but in her zippy strappy gold and black concoction, Gloria might have been dressed for a night on the town. Dressed to dazzle, to lure, entice, entrap. Maybe it was last night's outfit. Maybe Gloria hadn't been to bed but neither her face nor her clothes looked crumpled enough to have been on the go so long. The black bits of her outfit didn't have the linty, lived-in look which black took on faster than any other colour.

Black is not a colour.

Bridget opened her paper and skimmed the leaders. The Pope had just flown into visit some of Britain's trouble spots. The PM had just flown out to visit some of Central Europe's trouble spots. Prince Charles was yet again extolling the virtues of organic farming. The Russians were remaining adamantly belligerent towards Chechnya.

Like a heavy animal shaking itself out of sleep, the train

jolted into action, rapidly picking up speed. The headlines jumped. Suburban stations blurred by, places Bridget would never visit. Her trips north were always terminus to terminus. Unlike Gloria's crisp and glittering outfit, Bridget's black T-shirt and jeans had picked up crumbs from breakfast and flecks of dust and grit from the tube journey to King's Cross. The palms of her hands were streaked with grimy sweat. The back of her neck prickled. No matter how often she washed, she never felt properly clean in London. Hard water, that's what it was, the crummy tidemark it left on the sink and the bath, like flakes of dead skin. Hard water, hard streets.

Black is not a colour. A tone, a shade, a shadow. Umbra, penumbra. You cannot find black in the spectrum.

Miss Friar had reminded the class of this wearily, fluttering her pale eyelashes is if she'd been making the point since she was born. Friar Tuck, the girls called her: a lame joke. Tall, willow-thin Emily Friar bent like a sapling in the wind. The long, floating scarves which she attempted to loop aesthetically round her neck invariably unravelled as she went about the thankless task of trying to instil in her girls an appreciation of ART.

– You should never say you don't *like* a work of art. You just don't *understand* it, she'd whisper as she ushered a class round the Kelvingrove Art Gallery, a class of teenage girls whose only response had been to snigger at the nudes. Otherwise they trailed from one room to another, gossiping and bitching and eyeing up any men they came across. When Miss Friar approached, scarf fluttering behind her like an afterthought, hairpins working their way loose from her bird's nest of a bun, somebody would always pipe up:

– I don't *understand* that painting. I really don't *understand* it.

Relieved that her efforts had not been entirely in vain, Miss Friar would retreat, undulating, and prepared to infiltrate another class cluster. Emily Friar, her long hands twitching like fish as she enthused about Botticelli and Rembrandt, Cézanne and Matisse. Neither liked nor understood. Not hated. She was too flimsy, too ethereal to inspire hatred. Dead by now, no doubt.

Amidst the cloying odours of polish and adolescence, the clatter of school shoes and laughter echoing round the stuffy, high-ceilinged rooms, Bridget had stopped in front of a painting by Rembrandt: *Self Portrait with Cap, Gorget and Gold Chain.* Above it, a sign: On Loan from Italy. At first it was the chain she'd been interested in, because it looked so much like real gold, as if the artist had cheated and used some of the leaf which gilded the heavy, ornate frame. Close up though, it was just paint: yellow, white and a brown Miss Friar would have called Umber or Sienna, burnt or raw. Close up, Bridget had quickly lost interest in the chain. The face above it was not just life-like but alive, as if it would be warm to the touch if you broke the rules and stretched out a hand, a face which even in youth was wise, compassionate, perplexed.

– Mind if I smoke?

Gloria stuck a cigarette in her mouth and lit up. Her nail polish and lipstick were a pearly, pinky white.

– Want a beer? I've tons.

Gloria exhaled a jet of smoke.

– Always prepared, me. Like the boy scouts. Don't know what they're prepared for, mind, apart from helping old ladies across the road. Those silly shorts! I tell you, I'd know I was well past it if any of them came near me.

Gloria pulled a second can from her gold holdall.

– Sure you won't?

– It's a bit early for me, said Bridget.

– Early for me too, pet, but after what I've been through this morning, I reckon I deserve it.

Gloria tapped a shell-like ellipse against her can. Her fingernails bore little resemblance to Bridget's clipped, matte ovals.

– I look like an Eskimo, don't I? I look like Björk.

You weren't supposed to say *Eskimo* anymore. Inuit or some special tribal name was the currently acceptable terminology. Or was it First Nation? And Björk was from Iceland. Björk was Icelandic. Gloria had a broad, pleasant face, with narrow blue eyes and high cheekbones. Apart from the fact that she was blonde, there was some similarity.

– I quite like Björk, said Bridget.

– I like her too, pet. I just don't want to look like her. Funny little thing. Terrible taste in clothes… My Eskimo look won't last, by the way. Couple of days and I should be back to normal.

Now that the morning sun was slanting through the filthy windows, Bridget could see, beneath Gloria's heavy make-up, discoloration around the eyes, the yellows and blues of bruising.

– Björk's mad, Gloria continued. Of course everybody up there's mad. It's the latitude: all that darkness in the winter, then all that daylight in the summer. Does something to the brain, that.

– SAD, said Bridget.

– You what, pet?

– Seasonal Affective Disorder. SAD for short.

– Right, said Gloria. Knew it had a name. SAD. SAD mad. Quite good, that.

–Not really, said Bridget. Not at all.

Cath, Bridget's sister, who'd moved to the north western tip of Scotland, had been in the grip of SAD for years. At least that's what the doctors said, as if giving something a name made it less of an enemy.

Black is not a colour. A tone, a shade. Umbra, penumbra.

Light and shade. But more and more shade. Even in the height of summer, under the midnight sun, a heavy blanket of darkness smothered her sister. From time to time a finger of light would poke through and Cath would call. Her voice bright and brittle, she'd rattle off plans to sort the house, tackle the weeds in the garden, take up a hobby – had she really said *flamingo* dancing, or had it just been a bad line? Cath's plans would pour down the phone in a rush, a flood.

– One thing at a time, Bridget used to say, One day at a time. Realistic goals. She didn't say that any more, just listened, damming Cath's flow with: Good, that's good, that's really good. Are you getting out at all? Are you going to the beach?

Cath did, after all, live beside one of the most unspoilt stretches of coastline in the country.

As kids they'd both loved the seaside. Beaches were big enough territories to share. Cath built castles, Bridget searched for mussel and oyster shells; anything pearly. Abalone was what she'd been after. Mother of pearl. She knew abalone didn't like icy northern waters, but never gave up hope that through some fluke, some warm current, she'd be poking around in the tidal debris and there one would be, waiting for her. Abalone, abalone – over and over she'd say the name until it stopped being a word and became, instead, a caress, a lapping wave of sound; magical, intimate, meaningless. And somehow sad, the sound lifted by the breeze and tossed into the bay, like a mother calling for a lost child.

Bridget never did find abalone and she never found a pearl, though people did, from time to time. Of course, for an oyster, a pearl was not the point. A pearl was an abnormal growth, like a cyst, or tumour; benign perhaps, but not an essential part of an oyster's existence.

The train whizzed north, the sprawl of greater London thinning out, sooty brick and cement giving way to patches of green, the occasional black and white cow. People were beginning to wriggle out of their seats and trail to and fro from the buffet, swaying down the aisles as if they were at sea. The compartment livened up with the smells of coffee, burgers and tangerine peel, the snap of styrofoam cartons, crackle of crisp packets, the hiss of ring-pulls. Gloria stubbed out her cigarette and pressed her fingers to her discoloured cheeks.

– It'll be worth it in the end, she said. Better be. Cost me my car. Bloody good car too.

– What did?

– Me eye bags, pet. Getting rid of me eye bags. Got the staples out this morning.

That's why I look like Björk... You OK? You've gone a bit green.

– I'm fine, fine. What kind of car did you have?

– Porsche.

– Nice. And where are you heading for?

– Darlington.

Anything to get away from talking about staples.

Cath standing in front of the mirror, giggling at the mess she's made of her face, giggling, screeching, that hideous frantic screeching. Cath and her sick bloody sense of humour.

Gloria had a shop which sold costume jewellery. Fab Fakes. Business was brisk. She found out what people wanted and made sure she had it glittering in her window display.

– I've two mannequins for the body jewellery, one white, one black – well more of a cappuccino, really. Paid a local artist to do them for me, with holes in every possible place – apart from, you know, down there. I drew the line at that. Had to. Had to put knickers on them, too. The local vice squad paid me a visit. *These are works of art*, I said. *Works of art are meant to be naked.* But they wouldn't buy it. Said they'd do me for indecency, me! So the mannequins are in knickers. Leather thongs actually. Spoils the effect, I say, but there it is. Don't go in for piercing myself, apart from the old lobes. Too much of a coward, me. But you have to keep up, I mean, that's why you read your paper, isn't it, to keep up? And here's me chuntering on.

Bridget had only bought a paper to pass the time. She'd a lot to pass before she got to Cath's dusty, smelly cottage and once she was there, time would ache by, minute by minute. Cath didn't pass the time. Time passed Cath. It slipped by, ignoring her, crawling on like a dull determined slug, day to night, spring to summer.

– You've been good company, I'll say that, said Gloria. I was sat beside a right miserable git on the way down. Kept twitching and giving me funny looks. Course I had me shades on. Five in the morning and pitch black outside. Must have thought I was a nutter but I still had the staples in, see.

Cath'd had a fling with staples. She'd had a fling with a number of sharp and/or hot objects. After one too many visit to A&E, Dr Fish, the consultant psychiatrist, hauled her in. Cath refused to see him without Bridget being present. Dr Fish was a quiet-spoken man with a cool handshake and weary grey eyes.

– You're all sick, Cath said. Twisted.

After an hour or so of gently probing questions, Dr Fish ventured, hesitantly, that sex, or the lack of it, might be contributing to Cath's condition.

– Are you making me an offer?

Cath had always been quick off the mark. Until Dr Fish saw no option other than to slow her down, put her into permanent low gear.

Before going for the train, Bridget had spent an hour in the Rembrandt room at the Courtauld. An hour with the Rembrandts – and only a handful of other gallery-goers – before the long weekend with Cath, a calm, quiet hour sitting on the bench which ran down the middle of the room. Most of the paintings were self-portraits: Rembrandt's best subject was himself. From the artist as a young man through middle to old age, the same face on which life had deepened the scores and shadows around the eyes, accentuated the forlorn and increasingly sorrowful gaze.

The train was passing through some woods, fretted pines, zebra-striped birch with shimmering gold leaves. The sky, until then a dense, cement grey, began to darken. In the middle of the woods, the train was slowing down. As it ground to a halt, the rain began. A sigh flapped through the carriage like a slow broad-winged bird then settled in anticipation of the inevitable announcement.

– I had an hour's delay on the way down, said Gloria. Rabbits on the line. Rabbits! Almost missed me appointment because of rabbits on the line. I'd have had to go around like the bride of Frankenstein for another week! That surgeon's a busy man.

People were beginning to fidget, flip open laptops, poke at mobiles. And to moan.

– Might at least put us in the picture.

– I'm flying next time. Enough's enough.

– Can't get a signal.

– It's the trees. Trees, hills, scenery basically, screws up the signal.

– Dead time. Nothing but dead time.

Ping. Ping. Crackle.

– Good afternoon, ladies and gentlemen. We regret to announce that this train will be delayed due to a body on the line. As we will have to wait until the appropriate authorities arrive and carry out the necessary procedures, we may be here for some time. We would like to apologise for the delay. We also wish to advise passengers that the suicide victim – a young man – has been severely mutilated and the sight may cause distress.

Ping ping.

A chill passed through the compartment, an icy draught. People hunched up, hugged themselves, put on their jackets. Gloria wept loudly, tears and mascara dripping down her swollen cheeks.

Eventually, conversation limped into motion again, words inching forward, words which couldn't remain unsaid, sealed off, words which had to be released, dropped into the pool of shared experience, diluted.

– A young man. A young man. His life ahead of him.

– Did he know the train was due?

– The driver must have been in some state.

– Relatives, friends. Somebody's going to have to identify him.

– Pretty woods. Such pretty woods.

– How long does it take for a person to become just a body? How long does the soul stay around? Does it leave the body at the moment of death or does it wait and watch, stand guard? For how long?

– I know we're not supposed to, but I'm going to have a look. I've never seen a dead body before.

Gloria snivelled and smoked and looked out of the window. Bridget wrapped her arms tightly around her chest. Her body was in shock, rebelling against her mind's pretence of being in control. If she moved, she'd throw up. How stupid she'd been, wondering why the flow of red-eyed passengers had been to the back of the train rather than the front. Of course the driver wouldn't have had time to stop at that speed, of course the train, the entire intercity express must have... Of course the body was now at the back of the train.

Dead time. Time no more than a gap, a blank, an absence, a hole through which a life has slipped. A lost soul...

– I will never kill myself. Never. No matter how bad things get, living's better than... living's better... It wasn't a person anymore. I won't tell you what it was like...

But the lad in the Reebok shorts who slumped back into his seat couldn't help itemising every mutilation – fingers here, part of a leg there, insides outside, blood and guts on the tracks...

he had seen and now he had to tell. Gloria stood up and leaned over the back of her chair.

– Shut up, will you, she said. Just shut up.

– It's just... it was so awful... you didn't see...

– We've all got an imagination, pet.

It took nearly three hours before all the formalities were attended to, before the mutilated body was gathered together and bundled up in a waterproof bag, packed into the ambulance and driven away. It would be dark by the time Bridget reached Cath, country blackness and long past dinner time, not that there was likely to be any food to speak of. Would she tell Cath the reason for the delay, or palm her off with engine trouble? Nobody cheered when the train eventually started up, though everyone was glad to be moving again, to be going somewhere, glad simply to be alive. But it was a cautious gladness over which the shadow of sodden woods would always fall.

Black is not a colour. A tone, a shade, a shadow. The absence of light.

Salvage

A WOMAN WAS moving out of her city flat. As she was moving to a smaller place, the time had come to do a really good clear out, to part with some of the mishmash of bits and bobs passed on by her late parents or left behind by her children who'd grown up and moved away. Things had gathered around her unnoticed, like a small forest, dense but reassuring. She sold some of the more valuable items, gave to friends, lugged bags to charity shops and eagerly looked forward to rubbish nights. The process turned out to be less painful than she had anticipated. Now and then a child's favourite egg cup or dog-eared story book would prompt a few tears to spring hotly from her eyes but all in all she felt lighter. Moving house was a leave-taking, a shedding of skins.

It was tiring work, though, and the night before the removal van was scheduled to arrive, a residual miscellany still lay around awaiting disposal. The painting – one of her daughter's art college pieces – was hard to part with. It was good enough – if on the gloomy side for the woman's taste – but simply too big for the small flat into which she was moving and the even smaller flat her daughter now shared with her boyfriend.

If she'd had more time and energy, she might have been able to find a good home for it but she was low on both so it was with some regret that she put it out on the pavement, propped it against the wild tangle of honeysuckle, clematis and ivy sprawling over the fence. To prevent it tipping over and being trampled on by somebody stotting home from the late-night pub on the corner, she wedged the canvas between the fence and a couple of bags of rubbish. As if it mattered. When the bin men came in the morning it would no doubt be lobbed into the chute, crushed and mangled along with everything else.

Head down, lost in her thoughts, a student was making her way home. The sweet night scent of the honeysuckle made her pause and look around. Like many students, her accommodation was spartan and she could always do with interesting items to liven it up. Free items in particular. She turned the canvas over and came face to face with a stark monochrome composition, a noirish kind of thing with a single figure set back from what appeared to be a tall tenement window.

The student didn't know much about art – biology was her chosen subject, though that night she was regretting her choice – but the atmosphere of the painting appealed to her. She often felt gloomy and noirish, especially on nights when the air had turned cold and damp and the darkness had come down sooner than expected. Her boyfriend was off on a bloody rugby weekend and she had a fucking hellish essay to write. She picked up the painting and marched off along the road with her find. Being so big, the canvas was awkward to carry but she persevered, intending to use it to cover up some of the hideous wallpaper in her room, a repeating pattern which reminded her of coffins.

At the end of the street she stopped by a lamppost and held

the painting up to the light. The figure was male, a vague, shifty sort of male. The eyes had a blankness which reminded her of her boyfriend when she brought up the subject of the future. When she thought about it, having a version of him on the wall while she tussled with an essay and he was off on the piss with his mates wasn't such a great idea. As she turned the corner, a sudden gust of wind caught her find and slammed it against her face. A nail grazed her eyebrow. Instinctively she dropped the painting beside a nearby pile of rubbish. Was she bleeding? Would she need a tetanus injection? She went on home, gloomy and noirish but determined to sort something out. The boyfriend, the essay on infectious diseases. Either. Both.

Later that evening the woman who was about to flit put out a couple more bags of rubbish. Discovering that the painting was no longer where she left it and realising that somebody must have liked it enough to cart it off to wherever they were going, cheered her up and gave her the rush of ruthlessness she needed to undertake the final stage of clearing out.

It wasn't the best part of town for finding good stuff, not wealthy enough for a start but, as the junk dealer didn't need to remind himself, things often turned up in unexpected places. His van was parked a couple of streets away, in front of the pub where he'd just done a bit of business. With any luck. Bloke he'd got talking to was looking for a bookcase – who wasn't in this well-read city? By the sound of it, he had the very thing in the back shop. Solid oak. None of your stripped pine crap. Needed a bit of renovation but that's what the punters liked.

So far the junk dealer's stroll round the neighbourhood had come up with bugger all. A couple of beat-up kitchen cabinets which must have looked like rubbish when they were new, never mind twenty years on, some pocked kitchen chairs not worth the bother of stripping. But that canvas was in good nick. Properly stretched, no bulges or buckling. And the painting itself – he'd seen worse. A lot worse. He'd sold a lot worse. Sold some total shite to happy chappies. But old shite. Never handled any contemporary artwork.

He quite liked the look of the grey-faced guy lurking in the shadows, surrounded by fuzzy monochrome blocks. It made him think of dark winter days when he was stuck in the shop with his rescued wardrobes and tallboys, up-ended pews and free-standing doors, listening to some radio play and waiting for someone, anyone to poke their nose in the door. The junk business wasn't as brisk as he'd have liked but maybe the painting might help bring in one or two artsy punters. And he did know how to make anything sound like a bargain. A desirable bargain.

Balancing the canvas comfortably in the crook of his arm – the junk dealer knew how best to carry all sorts of awkward objects – he began to feel quite philosophical, even optimistic. After all, there had to be bad times to appreciate the good times. Bloke in the pub might well relieve him of the bookshelves and maybe even find something else to his liking. Tomorrow he'd pull out all the oak stuff. Display it to advantage.

The junk dealer carried the painting back along the road it had travelled earlier that evening, in the arms of the biology student. It flapped softly against the flat of his hand. The night air was sweet with the smell of hops from the brewery. It was a smell he loved – not for the association with beer, he was more of a whisky man – but it always made him think of somewhere quaint and rural and nostalgic, where greenery swayed lushly overhead and women were smiling and soft-bodied and the light was always golden. Then he caught the stink of rubbish: a rotting chicken carcass, cat litter, nappies? Further on, something nice again, something sweet, heady. He laid down the painting against railings draped in a thick mantle of creepers; ivy, clematis and a rampant honeysuckle in full bloom. He plucked a hand of honeysuckle, pink and fleshy under the streetlight. He stuck it in his buttonhole and walked on, abandoning the painting. After all, the shop was already chock-a-block with stuff which needed shifting.

In the morning the refuse van wheezed to a halt. The driver and his crew hit the street and began to feed rubbish bags, defunct electric fires, battered lampshades and stained mattresses into the crunching metal jaws. The painting, swaddled in a soft travelling rug retained for the purpose, was expertly slipped behind the seat. For some years, the head driver for the Central Division of the Cleansing Department had been quietly salvaging discarded works of art and was considered by some of the more adventurous private galleries, to know a good thing when he saw it.

Sheltered behind her hedge of fragrant creepers, the woman who was about to flit slept soundly and dreamed of bright, vacant rooms and an unfamiliar view from the windows. Not until nearly lunchtime, when the removal men banged insistently on her door, did she wake up.

Agnes

PICKED UP IN a junk shop for a song, passed on when my parents modernised their living room, she looks at me with the same intransigence as my daughter, the same glaze of adolescence highlighting her forehead, eyelids, the tip of her nose, her lip, her chin. Pierced ears, a thin ribbon knotted at the neck, the low cut collar of her dress emphasising the swell of budding breasts. Insolent, sullen, bored, or simply absenting herself from the undrawn place where she sits?

The frame is chipped, flaking, the glass greasy. Experts warned against cleaning in case, in the process, I ruined her: the chalk and the glass had already spent two hundred and thirty years rubbing along nicely; it might be a tricky business to prise them apart.

The question is: When I'm old and my daughter is middle-aged and it's time to pass things on, should I have my girl restored or let her be, luminous and grubby?

Learning to Fall

NOT AGAIN. *Hi Ho Silver Lining* kicking off yet another Sunday morning session. One of these days Kev really was going to floor TT, kick the blades from under him just as he was embarking on yet another of his once-famous cross-your-heart spins. Choosing the music wasn't his job but TT liked to have a finger – or toe – in everything.

Hi Ho

Not even TT's era. Skiffle was TT's era. Skiffle, yeah, TT was a skiffle kid and look at him now, in the harlequin cardigan and twill trousers, cradling the big belly proudly, as if he were carrying something other than excess weight, spinning like a top, the lambswool diamonds blurring into barcodes.

In the staffroom Kev checked his pigeon-hole, hoping that some of this season's fees had come in. There was only a circular about the Christmas party. Summer was barely over and the manager was trying to gee up the instructors into volunteering to do novelty turns. Another futile attempt to boost morale and encourage team spirit. Kev sucked down a quick cigarette while he took his skates and gloves from his locker. His stomach growled in response to the stink of sliced sausage from the café and perished rubber from the refrigeration system. He hadn't managed to fit in breakfast. Beginners on an empty stomach – Kev was no stranger to that particular form of self-punishment. He stubbed out his cigarette on the no-smoking sign and tossed the dowt in the bin.

They were on the ice already, an apprehensive huddle, clutching the rink-side like shipwrecks, wishing, hoping, praying possibly, that if they stayed very still, a non-slip surface would materialise in place of the hacked-up, water-logged ice which made their blunt hire skates skitter out from under them if they so much as blinked. A new class. Kev didn't need to wave or smile. Yet.

Twenty or so, mostly female by the looks of them, on the far side of the pad. Before he put on his gloves, he ran a hand over his chin. A shave was something else he hadn't managed to fit in but that was maybe all to the good. Stubble, along with the faded Levis and beat-up leather jacket, made him look rugged. So one of last term's bright-eyed students had told him. Jenny, was it? He was useless with names. Too many new faces to put names to. Janie, Janice, Janine? God knows. Tall, long-boned, awkward in her body, like a scarecrow on the ice and chatty with it, a nervous tongue tripping ahead of itself. Jeannie. Definitely Jeannie. Hadn't signed up for Continuing Beginners.

Ragged was what he felt, with a bitter knot of remorse sitting hotly in his gut. Getting rat-arsed on a Saturday night was stupid, but on a Saturday night Kev could resist anything except temptation. As TT had pointed out to him more than once, if he'd put aside half the money he spent unwinding, he could have done what he always talked about, packed up and taken off for Canada or Alaska, somewhere with ice worth lacing up the boots for, where you could smell trees and woodsmoke and glide between snowy mountains instead of ads for Paintball,

Go-Karting, cheap MOTs and Rock Steady Crowd Control.

Yeah well. Tommy Turnbull had been circumnavigating this poxy frozen oval a good few years longer than he had. And Jesus Mary McNicoll, with his gold earring, gelled Renaissance-look ringlets and Le Coq Sportif sweatshirts, may have spent a couple of seasons in Quebec but he, too, was in with the bricks now, in with the crumbling masonry and peeling paintwork, the stained concrete and spongy rubber.

Hi Ho Silver Lining

Kev flexed his gloved fingers and stepped on to the ice. Building up speed rapidly, he carved a long cool slice between TT and Jesus Mary and pulled up sharply in front of his new recruits, relishing the mixture of shock and awe he read on their races. A flash stop always got their attention. Impressed. Showed you could cut it, do the business. And Kev could, Kev really could do the business, he could've been, could've been... hmmm. Could've been an also ran in the championships and now yet another bunch of Sunday morning beginners was waiting to be shown how to take their first steps on ice.

Plenty of them at least. More money. Per capita payments. Blades on ice. It was a numbers game and who was he to complain if most of his students harboured fantasies about birling round the rink in gauzy skirts, partnered by lithe, sequinned pansies from Prague or Budapest. Kev's eyes skimmed the class: a dozen women, togged out in anoraks and fleeces and thermal gloves, a handful of men, dads with sons in tow, doing their Sunday morning duty; a slouch of skinny, pre-pubescent girls, in variations of the same baggy sports outfit, hair tied in high pony tails and bouncing bunches, or pegged out with complicated arrangements of shiny clasps. Heads like obstacle courses, outside and in. On a good morning, he'd endeavour to make eye contact with everybody but not today. Today it was the unfocused, all-inclusive smile.

– OK folks, hello there. I'm Kev Mallingray, your neighbourhood instructor, the boy who's been hanging out on this slippery surface since he was so high. And I'm telling you, I've seen a lot of folk do a lot of stupid things on the ice. Skating's a great activity *but* – and this is a but to be ignored at your peril – ice is cold and ice is hard and a bad fall hurts like a four letter word I'd rather not use in front of the ladies.

He had them. Had them holding their breath, gritting their teeth, girding their loins. He ran through what the introductory session would include: stance, balance, moving forwards, moving backwards, starts and stops, skating on one leg. He paused, allowing for the inevitable giggles as they pictured themselves doing arabesques. All Kev meant was raising a boot six inches above the surface. It was good to get a laugh though, and sometimes he'd spin out his stock-in-trade banter for the best part of the first session. But he wasn't in the mood to entertain. Wasn't in the mood to be there at all. The hangover didn't help, nor did TT's choice of music blaring out over the rink but what really chafed was an even more persistent irritant.

Darla, TT's first private pupil of the day was skating towards her instructor. She was dolled up as usual in white ski pants, a tailored black jacket and white leather gloves. After months of individual instruction from TT, she still skated like a block of wood, chin out like the prow of a boat, purple mouth a wedge of concentration. Given a choice of instructor, Darla wouldn't have gone for TT. Jesus Mary, who was in the middle of his balletic sex-on-legs routine and attracting surreptitious glances from Kev's beginners, yeah, Jesus Mary would have been the man for Darla. Even if she'd fancied a bit of rough and rugged, Kev didn't get a look in these days. Only Jesus Mary, great white hope for the championships and Tommy Turnbull, cupwinner turned coach, only they got their pick of the private pupils. Kev was the fall-back, the fill in, the slush pile sifter.

– Excuse me, I was wondering, could you…

Anxious, wrinkly smile. Hat like a tea cosy. Grey hair curling out from under it. Jogging suit, fleece, mittens.

– Could you teach us how to fall?

– Oh yes, that's what I was wondering, too...

– It would be handy to know that. The first thing they teach you at judo, isn't it, how to fall.

All it took was one nuisance to get them all gabbing away and having visions of slipped discs, smashed knees and dislocated elbows, of scans and x–rays and hobbling about on crutches. Tea Cosy looked pleased with herself. Kev's head throbbed.

– Good question, love. What's your name?

– Alice. Alice Pinks.

– First names will do.

First names were more than enough.

– So, Alice. You know, a lot of people ask me that very same question.

Stretching the truth – it had come up a couple of times – but the situation didn't demand truth. Class control was the objective.

– How to fall safely, Alice? Easy. Just don't.

Laughter from everyone except Tea Cosy, whose cheeks flushed and mouth puckered.

– Any more questions before we begin? Right, then, let's get to work.

On automatic pilot, Kev demonstrated the basic stance, knees slightly bent, feet in a v, arms like snow-heavy branches of a Christmas tree. He showed them the small tight steps they should try to take and sent them off on their first expedition across the ice.

Kev kicked the traffic cones into a line, cordoning off the beginners from the fast, counter-clockwise flow on the rest of the rink then skated to the far side, to watch his ice virgins wobble towards the barrier. They were doing OK, staying upright and advancing in a similar direction, all except a man and boy who had become stuck on the pad, unable to move forward.

The man was moving his feet but going nowhere. The boy just stood and scowled at the ice.

Once Tea Cosy Alice and her Learning to Fall Support Group had safely made it to the barrier, Kev swung round the edge of the rink and skimmed in behind the man and boy. A word in the ear, a light hand on the arm, it didn't take much, just a smidgeon of personal attention, some coaxing and cajoling, maybe even a bit of gentle bullying to see them through the impasse, the frozen moment. Well, that was the theory. The father's head was nodding mechanically but he was still walking on an imaginary treadmill. The boy was growing roots.

– Just take it easy. I'll be right back.

Kev whisked himself over to the barrier where the others were buzzing: they'd made it, they'd crossed the ice!

– Right, so you can all move in a forward direction. Roughly speaking. Now I'm going to show you how to skate backwards.

Women whooped with girlish excitement, girls gave each other doubtful, sidelong glances, men and boys adopted business-like frowns. Kev glanced back. The marooned father and son were still upright. He ran through the backstep routine. Tea Cosy was trying to catch his eye. Kev could see her mouth open, the next question lined up, ready to spill out as soon as he'd finished his spiel. Kev avoided her eager gaze: she'd had her say. He addressed his instructions directly to the teenage girls who, as he'd hoped, were too self-conscious to meet his eye.

– OK folks. You learn to skate by skating, not by talking about it, so off you go. Just remember: duck feet forward, hen toes backward. Spread out and take your time.

Barry White next and after Barry it would be Abba and after Abba... The class began to slither backwards. Tea Cosy crumpled up as if the pot had been taken out from under her.

– Don't try too hard, Alice. That's the secret. Let your skates do the work.

– Yes. Thank you, she replied, a quaver in her voice.

– Keep trying. Effort always gets results. In the end.

After Kev had made his way down the line, correcting backs, knees, ankles, chins, elbows, he nipped back to the man and boy.

– Getting a bit lonely out here, are we?

The boy's face was a thundercloud of embarrassment, rage and fear. The man's was blotchy; his breathing fast and shallow.

– I can't feel my feet, said the man. I'm not cut out for this.

– Cut out for it? Nobody's cut out for it, pal. If we'd been meant to travel on ice, we'd have been born with blades in our feet.

The boy gave a thin, grudging snigger. Kev spun them a couple of skating jokes, got them to lighten up, loosen up.

– That's more like it, people. Where would we all be without ice-breakers, eh? Now watch my feet. Don't think, just watch and copy me.

He demonstrated the step again then flipped to backstep so he could see them, as once more, they attempted to propel themselves forward.

– Way to go! Much better, much better. Both of you. Just keep at it, right. When you get to the barrier, you can walk off the ice and never go near it again. Lucky people, you have that option. But when you get there, the ice'll look a whole lot different. Trust me.

Kev skated towards the cones, closely watching the ragged, knock-kneed line skating backwards towards him, the father and son now creeping forward, making their hesitant marks on the heavily scored ice. Behind him, Kev heard the rasp of skates skidding to a halt. Before he could turn to see who was invading his space his blades were knocked from under him, his arms and legs windmilled and there was nothing he could do to avoid the thud of impact, the rush of white noise, the crackling blackness.

As the ceiling lights swam slowly back into focus and the slush seeped into his jeans, pain began to ring its alarm bells all over this body and hangover kicked in again with a vengeance. He had to get up, to smile, think of a joke to tell his Sunday morning beginners about falling, to turn a disaster into a demonstration. But first, somebody was about to get a bollocking.

Using the official safety method, Kev stood up and slapped the crushed ice off his jeans. A few feet away, a wee boy with blazing cheeks dug his hands in his pockets and stared at the spot where Kev had fallen. Kev took a firm hold of the boy's arm.

– Sorry, Mister.

– You will be if you don't learn to stop properly.

– New skates, said the boy. Breaking them in.

– Aye, well, I'll be breaking you in, son, if you come near me and my beginners again. Now get lost and stay lost... Good skates by the way. Too good for a toerag like you.

Released from Kev's grip, the boy belted off like a dog from a trap and was soon absorbed into the general swirl on the main body of the rink. TT, who, accompanied by Abba's *Mamma Mia* was instructing Darla in the rudiments of ice tango, waved smugly in Kev's direction and pulled his private pupil into as tight a clinch as his belly would allow. In the middle of the rink, a circle of admirers skated slowly round Jesus Mary McNicoll, agog at his twirls and arabesques.

After a deliberately showy piece of footwork, Kev pulled up at the barrier and turned to face his class. He rubbed his aching back and prepared to launch into an impromptu lesson: How to Get Up after a Fall. Most of them were still working their way backwards. Those who had reached the barrier were calling out encouragement to the others. The previously marooned father and son had their eyes resolutely trained on one of the rinkside ads. Kev smiled fondly at his Sunday morning beginners. They hadn't seen the kid crash into him. Hadn't witnessed his fall.

The Multicultural Fashion Show

WITH TIME TO spare before the highlight of their day, Elsie and
Rawinda, savouring the sun and each other's company, are
making a sedate tour of the municipal park. The air smells of
curry and late roses. They stop first at the food stalls, sniff at
the Madras and the Roghan Josh, the couscous and falafels,
smile at the jewel-coloured candies.

– Want to eat something? Rawinda asks.

– No, dear. I'm saving myself for later.

– Me too.

They move on, leaving others to pile paper plates with food.
At the jewellery stalls they linger and feast their eyes on intricate
necklaces, earrings, nose studs and bracelets. At one stall, a
girl with beaded braids twisted into a knot on top of her head,
appears to be wearing half her stock.

– It's a bit early but I could do my Christmas shopping
right here, says Elsie.

– I too could make my purchases for Divali.

– Looking for something in particular?

– No dear. Just looking, says Rawinda. Maybe we'll

come back later.

– If we survive the fashion show!

– You're lucky to get tickets, says the stallkeeper. It's a sell-out.

– Ah, but you see, we have friends in high places, says Rawinda.

– Aye, says Elsie. We're on intimate terms with some stars of the show.

Casting a last wistful glance at the jewellery, the two women move on to the fabric tents. Bolts of cotton and silk are stacked high above their heads. Elsie fingers a corner of damson silk, embroidered with blue and gold peacocks.

– Does that no take your breath away?

– Gorgeous. But look at this one. What colour would you call it... magenta, mauve, heliotrope? I get mixed up with names for the pinky purply colours.

– So do I, dear. And I'm no sure I'd ken heliotrope if I saw it. But it's bonny all right.

– Very fine. I haven't seen sari silk like this since – oh, long ago, too long ago.

– Too strong a colour for me but it would look a treat on you.

– Maybe too strong for me too, dear. I'm so pale nowadays. Like milky tea. Not enough sun here.

– Nice today, though.

– It is. And such a good turnout, says Rawinda.

– Even better than last year, says Elsie. A good sign. More folk wanting to join in. Makes you feel hopeful.

– Yes. My mother used to say hope was like chilli: a little goes a long way.

Rawinda lingers outside the travel agency tent, checking out the cheap deals to India. Elsie pauses to say hello to a sturdy pink-faced policemen, resting against the panda van. There's very little police presence in the park and what there is in this easy, ambling crowd is more of a PR exercise than a necessity.

– That laddie was at school with my daughter, Elsie says as they move on. A right bad lot too, as I remember. Always in trouble.

– He'll be plenty qualified for the job, then.

– Aye. Takes one to know one.

Music drifts across the park from a small open-air stage which has been erected on the far side, in front of a line of the trees.

–The dancers – we almost forgot about the dancers!

Rawinda checks her chunky digital watch, incongruous on the slender wrist emerging from the folds of an amethyst sari.

– We've time to take a look. It would be nice if the fashion show started on time but one thing is certain: it won't.

– What was it held up the show last year, some technical hitch?

– So many people behind the scenes too.

– Aye, and half of them relatives!

– I take no responsibility for my children's lack of organisation.

– Me neither. Let's go and see the dancers.

The two grandmothers pick their way across the grass to the far side of the park, pausing every now and then to admire a pretty child, well-scrubbed and spruced up for the day.

– It really is a lovely day, says Rawinda. People here complain about the weather – I do myself – but really I like it. Never boring like at home. Dry season, wet season. Hot and not so hot. At home there was no point in talking about the weather.

– Here some folk can't talk about anything else. Or don't want to.

– Mmm. But sometimes a pointless conversation is better than no conversation at all.

A tight crowd, several rows deep, has assembled around a brightly painted stage. Rawinda elbows her way towards the front.

– We oldies are allowed to be rude sometimes. Besides, all

the young people these days are so tall. We'll not see a thing if we don't push a little.

– Sorry, says Elsie, squeezing through the throng of tall young people.

– Much better, says Rawinda, planting her feet firmly at the edge of the stage. We can see now.

What they see is a girl of no more than ten or eleven, dressed in a glittering top and gauzy trousers. With a stack of pots balanced on her head, she is performing a complicated dance. Every so often she pauses and squats down, smiling and flashing her eyes alluringly. Each time, a bare-chested man, sporting a magnificent black moustache, adds another pot to the growing tower on her head.

– Ten pots, Ladies and Gentlemen. Now she's running. Eleven pots. Now she's hopping. Twelve pots. Now she's skipping...

A beautiful Indian woman in a leather jacket and designer jeans provides the commentary. At the addition of each new pot, the audience applauds. After fifteen pots the musicians strike up a dramatic drumroll. The dancer continues smiling as the compere announces:

– Now, Ladies and Gentlemen, now our newest girl is going to show what she's made of – by walking over hot coals!

Elsie blanches, clutches Rawinda's arm.

– I've seen enough, dear.

– But this is the climax. The true test of a dancer.

The drum roll stops and the crowd falls silent. From the back of the stage, the man with the moustache pulls forward a fireproof mat covered in glowing coals which crackle softly as they bump together. He spreads the mat over the stage. Then, with a pair of tongs, picks up an ember and spits on it. It hisses like a snake.

– I can't watch, Rawinda. I feel sick at the very thought.

– The girl will feel no pain. That is the point. She has gone through much training. She has achieved a state of mind over matter. The power of concentration, of will. Of faith.

– I can't watch. I just can't.

Elsie turns away abruptly and pushes back through the audience. Rawinda follows, catches up with her.

– Never mind, dear. We should probably make our way to the marquee now, anyway.

– Lovely dancer, says Elsie. And so young to be so skilful.

– At home girls start learning to dance as soon as they can walk. It's a living.

Elsie's head is pounding with embarrassment and annoyance. With herself. She doesn't have faith in mind over matter, the power of will. When she thinks about it, she doesn't have faith in anything much. Which makes her feel inadequate, as if she's failing her friend. And Rawinda has been a good friend to her, better than many.

– Sorry.

– No need to be sorry. Remember the haggis supper?

– That's different.

– Not at all. I had no faith whatsoever in the consequences of consuming that horrible-looking thing.

Earlier in the year it had been Elsie and Johnny's treat to take Rawinda and Jamal to a Burns' Supper complete with music and poetry and speeches. Rawinda had worn a tartan sari which everybody had admired. Jamal had thought about hiring a kilt but in the end had worn a suit and a tartan tie. Johnny and Elsie had tried their best to make sure nothing might spoil their evening. And nothing had until the man with the dagger stabbed the haggis and its blood and meal innards oozed on to the silver salver. The climax.

– Maybe some things you have to grow up with, dear.

– Aye.

On their way to the marquee, they stop in front of the beer tent where Johnny and Jamal are sipping beer and earnestly studying their cans.

– Comparing Tiger to Tennent's as usual.

– Should we drag them out?

– They'll come in their own good time.

– That's what I'm worried about. Mind, Johnny wouldn't dare be late for anything Celie's involved in. Thinks the world of his granddaughter.

– Jamal is just the same. Ayesha can do no wrong in his eyes.

Seeing the crowd gathered under the banner advertising the fashion show, Elsie and Rawinda begin to walk a little faster. Their grandchildren would never forgive them if they didn't manage to see the show on account of being stuck too far back, two small women in a growing world.

Their progress into the tent is blocked by an official-looking man speaking through a megaphone and ordering everybody to stand back.

– So much fuss.

– Too big for their boots.

They join a straggling queue behind a cluster of restless teenage boys in gleaming white dhotis and fancy trainers. Gulls swoop down on the rubbish bin, already filled to overflowing with juice cans and paper plates, the remains of dahl, chapatis and chips. Grass tickles their sandaled feet. A cool, salty breeze blows across the park.

– Not long until we'll have to look out our winter woollies.

– Cardies and thermal vests.

– Won't see many of *them* on show today.

– The young don't feel the cold.

– Hot blood.

– Hormones.

– When I was young I didn't know what hormones were.

– Me neither. Everything's out in the open now.

– A good thing too. People can die of ignorance.

– There they are!

– Always straggling.

– Late for their own funerals, if they had any say in the matter.

Two short, silver haired men, each clutching a beer can, trot towards their wives.

– Told you we'd be fine for time, says Johnny.

– What's causing the holdup? says Jamal.

– Nobody's said a thing, says Rawinda.

– Well, that's us moving now, says Johnny. Perfect timing, eh?

– Perfect luck, more like, says Elsie.

At the front of the queue, the man wiv- the megaphone has begun to usher people through a flap in the canvas. Two policemen, one on either side, using the arm movements normally employed for traffic control, are helping to speed things up. The queue obliges, filing through the narrow entrance into the hot bright tent. Inside, under the late summer sun, the air has baked and swollen and smells of warm canvas and trodden-down grass.

Elsie and Rawinda, a husband on either side, edge towards the nearest free seats to the stage, about half way back, in the middle of a row. After the delay, everybody is keen to sit down quickly and get on with what they came for: to watch their friends, their children and grandchildren do their stuff on the flimsy catwalk.

– We're putting bets on as to which of the girls is going to hit the big time first, says Jamal.

– Backing each other's offspring, of course, says Johnny.

– That way nobody will lose out, says Jamal.

– Jamal's booked a table at the Taj.

– We're going Dutch, says Jamal. Double, no triple Dutch actually.

– The stars get to eat free, mind, says Johnny. We're banking on the chance that in a few years they'll be able to treat us!

– It will be so nice to have everybody together, says Rawinda. Elsie shivers, hugs herself.

– You can't be cold, says Johnny. It's like an oven in here.

– It's just nerves. I keep thinking of silly little things that could go wrong: somebody tripping on stage, a sleeve coming off a jacket. Some of Celie's outfits were barely tacked together...

– Don't worry, says Rawinda. Haven't they been preparing for weeks?

– Months!

The chatter turns into applause as the man who'd earlier been in charge of the megaphone skips the length of the catwalk and takes the microphone from its stand.

– Could I have quiet, please? he says, several times.

Eventually the audience complies.

– Good afternoon, Ladies and Gentlemen, boys and girls. Great to see so many of you here to support our second year of the Multicultural Fashion Show. We have worked on the success of last year's very popular event to provide an even more ground- breaking show. On behalf of the organisers, I apologise for the delay but, unfortunately, just as we were putting the finishing touches into place backstage, we were informed by an anonymous caller that there was a bomb in the marquee.

Ripples of unease spread rapidly through the tent. The heat intensifies.

The door flaps have been closed and the exits are indistinguishable from the straining canvas walls. Nobody gets up but many turn in their seats, trying to locate the exits. A low, tense murmur hangs in the charged air. The fact that a bomb hasn't been found doesn't guarantee that there isn't one. And if somebody really wanted a device to go off, it wouldn't be left lying around in an obvious place. Everybody in the place knows this, except maybe the youngest children, who don't know what a bomb is and who are now being clutched tightly by the nearest relative.

– There is no need to panic, no need to panic! With the help of specially trained experts we have made a thorough search of the premises and have found nothing at all suspicious. We are convinced that this bomb scare is nothing more than a hoax. It is, we know, very distressing to think that some people take pleasure from such a sick joke but we can assure you that we have found nothing. And so we are about to start the show. A great deal of work has gone into this event and we hope you will enjoy it. So without further ado, Ladies and Gentlemen, boys and girls, let's get this place jumping!

Elsie's heart is beating hard, too hard. Her feet are on fire. Otherwise she feels nothing. She has become all beating heart and burning feet. Beside her, Rawinda is rigid, controlling her body as a means of controlling her fear. Mind over matter. But the colour has drained from her face, leaving only deep dark circles around the eyes, like bruises. Johnny and Jamal stare too intently at the empty catwalk.

The music starts, up-tempo Bangra blasting out of the speakers. Roaming spotlights splash pools of colour across the catwalk. Johnny, Elsie, Rawinda and Jamal hold hands, a small, silver-haired cordon against calamity. Elsie tries to imagine walking on hot coals and feeling no pain. And prays to any god who'll listen, for faith in the efficiency of specially trained experts. Rawinda blinks, wills herself to breathe slowly, leave her tinderbox of memories undisturbed. They all wait. And hope. Like everyone else in the marquee they know that they won't, now, enjoy a single moment of the show. They will, however, pay close attention for the duration in the hope that, if everyone is not blown to kingdom come they will, over a jubilant dinner at the Taj, be able to offer effusive and detailed compliments to all members of their precious families.

Sergei

– THE WEATHER IS permissive today, he said, licking his lips.
That leftover summer heat, the heavy sky incubating a storm.
It is especially sympathetic to gluttony, lust and sloth. Pride, in
its place, perhaps. But envy, avarice and wrath should be kept
under wraps.

Drops of warm rain prickled the skin of the pond where fat
carp rose, dipped back into the water and found a new place
to come up for air.

After a lunch of slippery dumplings, salty cheese and young
wine as brown and frothy as the Danube, he sat at the piano,
played a Chopin Mazurka and a Joplin Cakewalk. Stiffly.
Stumbled over the tricky bits. I stood at a tall window, peeling
a peach. Outside, leaves glittered like pirate gold. Lightning
tore through a pewter sky.

When rain streamed down the glass and blurred our view of
the elemental orgasm, we retired to his chamber for a game of

what he insisted on calling *Hunt the Sausage*. After, we slept until nightfall.

When I had to leave, he didn't even consider getting out of bed. Just flicked his eyes open, closed them again. Waggled three fingers. Smiled. Smudged lipstick bled into the creases around his mouth.

It was still pouring when I drove down the long, curving avenue of sodden lime trees. The wipers beat madly, like the wings of a trapped bird. I've never been back.

Raging Ladies 1979

– Hi there. Doris d'Annunzio, bringing you the latest on the meteorological front at seventeen hundred hours, Atlantic time. The anticyclone which originated in the Caribbean is gathering velocity as it moves north west through the Gulf of Mexico. From our satellite reports, it's too soon to make an accurate prediction as to the direction and scale of the storm but all the signs say keep on your toes; Hurricane David is on course to hit somewhere along our coastline around midnight tonight. State authorities say all coastal dwellers should be vigilant over the next twenty four hours, so keep tuned to our hourly update. For now, it's a beautiful sunny day out there, twenty-nine degrees and a light breeze off the water. Get yourself a frozen daiquiri or a long cool iced tea and chill out to our summer sounds. First off, Willie Nelson singing Blue Skies.

– Can you hear it?
   – Can't hear a Goddamn thing except the friggin treadmill. I so hate all the noise at the gym. We really should think about some outdoor exercise.

– It's a long way off. Sounds like nothing much yet.

– Did you take your heart rate today?

– Who needs it.

– Uh oh. So it's going to be one of those days.

– Saw it in my sleep last night. All those little red capsules blipping. The heart throbbing like an electric valentine.

– You're always a mess on angel dust.

– Some people think I'm a mess without it.

– Well, some people don't know shit.

– Can't you hear it, Connie? It's like a sighing sound.

– All I can hear is heavy breathing and these friggin machines. Why don't we take up hiking? Fresh air, nice boots…

– It's not working.

– That chest bench is a killer. Cripples me too.

– It's just not working.

– A bad attitude fucks you.

– I don't have a bad attitude.

– No. You don't have any attitude at all.

– She's gonna come, isn't she, Connie.

– He, sweetie. This time it's a he. David. First year a Raging Lady's been a he. Historic, huh?

– David. Good choice of name.

– A very popular choice. David is gonna hit town some place or other. Whether he makes it to the party's another question. Andrew's coming as Edna. Heaven only knows what kind of costume he'll come up with for *her*. Barry's coming as Betsey. He's got this beehive wig, kinda like the French aristocracy wore before they got their heads chopped off, with flashing lights through it. It's *fabulous*. Tommy's coming as Camille; white satin wedding dress with a huge lace train, sort of Wide Sargasso Sea/Virgin Islands thing. Sonny says he's been a girl too many times already so he's coming as a priest. Got his sister to sew *Is That All There Is?* over the cross on the back of his robe. Honey, it's gonna be wild. Even if David don't show.

– Wild. Yeah. Shit, I've less stamina now than months ago. And if you wanna talk muscle, man, it's been sucked right out of me.

– Paul, will you please cut the misery shit?

– It's getting louder. Still very far away but coming closer.

– You do the programme, take the medication. We take notes, we wait, we do not lose hope.

– You do what you like. All that energy. Round and round, like some kind of atmospheric treadmill...

– Please try. Pretty please?

– Lay off, nursie.

– We should go to the beach. Watch the boy hit town. He will be *devastating*!

– After all the fuss, he'd better make a grand entrance.

– Tommy's making Margaritas, Ramon's bringing his mama's hotter-than-hell stuffed chillies, Jesse got his aunt in Whiskey Creek to custom-pluck a dozen corn-fed chickens, Sonny's bringing ribs and black-eyed peas. I just love Sonny's ribs.

– Tell me about it.

– I can't make you laugh any more. I used to make you laugh.

– Don't start, Constantine, just don't start.

– If you wanna stay home tonight, just say so, OK? We can duck out, it's no big deal.

– I already told you, I don't wanna stay home.

– You never do these days. Out out out. Burning yourself up night after night and wondering why you feel like death the next day. Sorry about the D word but you need to take care of your body. Did you eat lunch?

– No. So?

– See how you are? You won't give yourself a chance. Maybe we should just stay home tonight. I don't mind missing the party, really. I'll cook, we can chill and watch TV. How about shrimp in garlic butter, hot sauce on the side, a Caesar salad...

– Food food food. I don't give a shit what we eat. I'm outta here.

– But you've hardly done anything. A workout's no good if you don't push yourself a little... where are you going?

– Home. To bed. To sleep.

– Want some company?

– I said sleep.

* * * *

– Hey, Constantine, you look so well! Still taking care of yourself, huh.

– I try, Georgia, I try. Somebody has to.

– It's like that is it? And how's the boy?

– So-so. And so irresponsible.

– You two have sure hung in there. People tell me you aint never without him these days.

– Well honey, I am right now. But he's precious. And you gotta take care of precious people or somebody else will step right in and take care of them for you.

– Yeah but cute boys – never a shortage around here. Whole new shoal comes in on the tide.

– You're such a bitch, you know that.

– And you love me for it, right?

– Most of the time, Georgie. Most of the time. Are you coming to the party?

– Am I coming? Honey, I been asked by special request to be your Mistress of Ceremonies! Now that's an honour I can't refuse. Spent all of last night sewing rhinestones on my jean jacket. My nails look like I've been gold-digging without a spade.

– Rhinestones. Let me guess. Dolly?

– Close, but not close enough. Tammy.

– All right! *Stand By Your Man*.

– If I could find me one with enough heterosexual tendencies, I just might think about it. Trouble is, every time I find me a man, I bring him down to meet you folks and what happens? I go powder my nose and when I when I get back from the bathroom my date's up on the dance floor shaking his stuff to YMCA, you know what I'm saying, honey…

– You know I'm sorry, Georgie.

– Don't be. You and me, shit, we're still friends, that's what's so great. If I lose a man to another woman, no way are we gonna be friends… So where is Paul?

– Home. Alone.

– You two been fighting?

– We don't fight. Not any more.

– No? Time was you'd lay into each other like a pair of red-headed stepbrothers.

– You been gone some. Is it good to be back?

– Too soon to tell.

* * * *

– Hi, sweetie. How's my sleeping beauty?

– Awake. And ugly.

– Tsk, tsk. Want me to wave my magic wand?

– Go screw, Connie.

– Hey now, don't go trashing your fairy godmother. Spirit people can turn real mean if you don't treat us nice.

– You can't touch me, man.

– Not the way I'd like to.

– Don't. Please.

– Sorry.

– Don't be. I don't want sorry. I hate it when you're fucking sorry.

– OK, I'm not sorry, not sorry, not sorry at all, I feel totally OK about everything I do being wrong. I don't give a motherfucking shit, OK?

– I don't wanna fight.

– Me neither. Jesus. Let's just take it easy. Sure you don't want to go to the beach? Get a little sun kissed?

– No.

* * * *

– Hi guys. Remember me? Your very own Southern Czarina. Are y'all having a good time? Sure you are. You guys always have a good time, right. This is one place in the world where nothing, and I mean nothing, will ever get in the way of a party. There's a mighty big wind out there, the first ever boy storm is a-roaring up against our coastline and here y'all are, just as I remember, still dressin up as Goddamn girls. I tell ya, next year I'm gonna make the break and come as a man. I'm gonna get me one of them snakeskin suits, a fedora. Maybe I'll even stuff the front of my pants with a little *surprise*... I heard that, honey. You never know your luck.

– Bring on the dancing girls, bring on the babes! Hey Georgie, when you're done being MC, let's dance. We haven't danced since way back.

– Love the pearls, darling.

– That's your fourth Margarita, Paul. On an empty stomach. Let me get you a plate of something? You're gonna fuck your liver.

– So my liver can get it on with rest of my organs. Relax, Connie. Smoke a bone. Drop a lude. Georgia's lookin good. Why did she come back?

– She didn't say. I haven't seen that necklace before. Who gave it to you?

– Did I say it was a present?

– It's not really something you could afford to buy for yourself.

– You're so right, Connie. Always right. Always on the nail. No, it's not something I'd buy for myself.

– Why do you do this to me?

– Don't torment yourself. I can't remember who gave me it. And it don't matter. Suits me, right?

– OK, ever'body, first on the floor an itchin to blow up a storm like she did back in 1954 – too long ago for some of you chirruns to remember but I was there, honey, I was there. And here she is, right now, let's hear it for Edna!

– My mother wore a hat like that on her wedding day.

– She must have looked *fabulous*.

– Her moment of glory. One single moment of glory in an entire lifetime. It's not enough.

– And now, folks, smashing into the mid-Sixties and doing one and a half billion dollars' worth of damage, move aside Edna, cos Betsey's gonna suck the wind right out of your sails.

– Don't you just love that headdress.

– He's close, really close. He's gonna raise the fucking roof, gonna blow it right off.

– What are you talking about?

– And now our third finalist. From 1969, one wickedly dangerous Creole Belle, come in Camille!

– *Here comes the bride, fifty miles wide.*

– Ain't she just a dream, guys?

– *Wind speed of up to three hundred miles an hour, sea and sky whipped into a spin.*

– I'm getting a bad feeling about this, Paul.

– So, guys, who d'y'all reckon's gonna be queen of the big winds tonight?

– *Boats tossed about like corks, trees bent to the ground like limbo dancers.*

– I keep thinking about that weather forecast, Paul. Around midnight, they said.

– *Wind that can drive a nail through a tree at the speed of a bullet.*

– We should go, Paul. We should get outta here.

– I want another Margarita. Get me another Margarita, Connie. Go on. Be a gentleman!

– Don't do this to me. We've seen the parade. Let's go. Let's go home, Paul. Please.

– Another Margarita. Margaritas on the house! I'm staying. I'm waiting, waiting for David.

Threadbare

A COUPLE WORKED away from home a lot. On one of their trips they brought back an intricately woven rug, brightly coloured with natural dyes squeezed from the petals of flowers, boiled from the roots and leaves of vegetables, ground from seeds and kernels. They were pleased with their purchase but didn't have time to appreciate it fully as not long after they returned from being away, they had to go away again.

Where in their pleasant, sunny flat the rug would look best was a decision which would have to wait until their return but they unrolled it anyway, admired it briefly, tried to figure out the story it was meant to tell, of man and animal, their vital but precarious relationship with the earth – at least that's what the rug seller's yarn suggested. After they had identified some of the emblematic animals and birds and giant moths and butterflies, they rolled up the rug again and slipped it carefully back inside its coccoon of brown paper.

All the clothes from their last trip had to be washed and their bags had to be packed again almost as soon as the laundry had dried. In between hanging several loads of washing on the line, they opened their mail and checked the messages on the answering machine. It was always faintly disappointing how little interesting communication awaited them on their return home. They replied to essential correspondence, mostly work-related, and made a few phone calls to friends.

As there was no food in the house and little time for shopping and cooking, and due to being paid a lump sum at the end of their last contract, they were feeling flush and ate takeaways every night. They would have been content to stay at home in familiar surroundings instead of rushing around, heads full of timetables and itineraries. The flat was comfortable and they'd got it as they liked it. As they were away a lot they didn't bother much about house plants – a cactus garden was all that survived months without watering – but they did have an interesting collection of textiles: rugs, cushion covers, curtains and wall-hangings, many of which they'd picked up on their travels.

Upping and offing so soon after returning home was a bit of a pain but everything went according to schedule and the trip turned out to be one of the best ever. The place was spectacular, the people friendly, accommodation comfortable, comestibles plentiful and affordable, the work challenging but rewarding. It was all so good that they considered extending their contract but eventually decided that, in spite of all the attractions, they wanted to be back home with their own belongings around them.

The return flight came in before dawn and first light was breaking as the taxi dropped them off at the flat. Mail was piled up behind the door so it took a bit of manoeuvring to open it. The hall smelled a bit musty as it always did when they'd been away but otherwise it was just as they had left it, the framed photos on the wall, the varnished floorboards. They left their bags in the hall and went through to the living room, each carrying an armful of envelopes.

What they saw was baffling. There were no longer any curtains on the window, only the plastic hooks hanging on the rail. The sofa had been stripped to its metal frame. Zips from cushions covers dangled between the springs like centipedes. A rubber slipmat was all that remained of the carpet. The rolled brown paper which had held the rug they'd brought back on their previous trip was as empty as a sloughed-off skin. Two plastic soles peeping out from under the skeleton of the sofa was all that remained of a pair of woollen slippers. One the wall where two silk tapestries had formerly hung, were two framed rectangles of nothing. The living room was stripped naked, a textile-free zone. It was only when they saw the moth carcasses, piled up in corners of the room like drifts of old leaves and they realised that the rug, in its brown paper wrapping had contained more than they'd bargained for, that the word *threadbare* took on a painfully personal significance.

Bitsy

I EXPECT SHE'D rather have been depicted in that mangy old fleece and that God-awful woollen headband she wears from October to March on account of her sensitive ears. Or bumbling about the kitchen in wellies and mud-coloured Barbour, up to her elbows in dog drool, spooning chunks of Pedigree Chum into plastic bowls. Playing hostess, handing round canapés at drinks parties is her idea of hell. She tells me often enough and after a gin or four doesn't give a damn who else hears. Bugger all I can do about it. Knew what she was in for when she married me. Never made out I had any intention of going in for the reconstructed male option when it came to domestic roles. The hairstyle's an improvement on her usual institutional bob – and have I ever complained about her spending money on her appearance? What else does she need to spend money on, for God's sake. But that dress – those ribbons, that fuss around the neckline – makes her look like some old-fashioned child at a party. Couldn't she have chosen something with a bit more class? As for that chap, that artist I paid good money to do her likeness, couldn't he have made her look a bit happier?

The dead shall live. The living die
And music shall untune the sky.
                                    DRYDEN

Mazzard's Coop

RABBITS AGAIN. OUTSIDE the gate, on either side of the street.
Could be roadkill, could have been thrown up by the wheels of
a passing car and landed there, just so, heads pointing north
and south. But you know those eternal burrowers are not
roadkill. You know how they got there, why they're there, know
they mean Della's been by, hexing the place.

As if a tinker's curse could bring you – or anybody else around
here – worse luck than you've had already.

But you're a gambling man, Mazzard. You, Jack and Willie
were all gambling men. A gambling man pays heed to signs,
doesn't underestimate Della's dirty tricks.

The day's been warm and sunny, grand for the kiddies' gala.
Wild garlic seasoning the breeze. The bunting draped between
the tight huddle of miners' rows fluttered and flapped. No
miners left in the rows now, of course. Even those, especially
those who hung on till the bitter, bankrupt end of the pit's

history couldn't begin to afford the inflated prices of the renovated dwellings. And how many who turned out to cheer the brass band as it paraded through the streets, trumpets and trombones flashing in the sun, would have had a clue what the fanfare signified? Incomers every one, with work elsewhere. Has to be elsewhere. Nothing left here.

In two minds about going anywhere near the gala but after a week of rain you'd felt restless, cooped up like your blasted birds. You needed to get out. The smell of wet birdshit hung over your house like a hooped net. You slapped the bunnet on the old head. Smooth as bone now. No more curls to charm the girls. You cleaned out the cage, changed the water, filled the food trays and set off on the walk you could do with your eyes shut, your personal stations of the cross: under the viaduct, along the riverbank where the water runs fast and high, across the bridge and down the concrete path which leads past the powerhouse, the pithead, the visitors' car park. Even as a museum, a showcase for Tilley lamps, embroidered union banners and the smiling black-faced camaraderie of yesteryear, the place once again is on the verge of going under. When it does, when the vast, grimy anachronism is eventually demolished and replaced by clusters of commuter homes in quaintly named cul-de-sacs, when the last traces of coal dust have been sluiced away, what will be left of it all, Mazzard? What will be left of that hellish quest for black diamonds?

Not always enough birds to go round, so some days you had to take a chance. Willie knew the odds. So did you.

Even before you reached the street party you knew it was a waste of time, knew your ties with the rows had been severed long ago. Jack O'Lantern, from next door, was there in the thick of it all, sat on a bench, dandling somebody's bairn on his knee. Jack's a familiar face, as familiar as could be, but you'd be lucky to get as much as a nod. Instead of edging into the sunny crush of folk enjoying themselves, you turned away from the brass band, the bunting, the bouncy castle, and took the main road home. None of the partygoers noticed you pass by. But you could feel the cardboard men at your back, all the way to your gate.

You could leave the rabbits for nature to take its course, for that buzzard circling high above your head to tear apart. Or next door's cats. But you can't be sure they're clean kill, can you? Can't be sure Della hasn't tampered with the carcasses. She knows her herbs and potions, knows what can be sprinkled on what and still taste safe. Even though there's no love lost between you and next door's cats, even if they're forever sniffing around the coop or crouching in the long grass by the burn, waiting for the chance to do their own killing, you wouldn't want them getting sick, would you, Mazzard? You wouldn't want Jack O'Lantern chapping the door of an evening because his beloved mogs had copped it from some tainted meat they found outside your place.

You and Jack go back a long way. You, Jack and Willie went back a long way. The pub on payday: bright-eyed from beer and freedom from work, The *Morning Star* in your pockets and rosy-tinted talk of the glories of Moscow, Beijing, Havana. The marches: hand-painted placards held aloft between you, linked arms as you trekked south, a united front, a wall against greed and injustice. The strikes: the divvying up of food, fags, firewood, when there was any to go round. Gala days – the real thing: the three of you scrubbed and shaved and gleaming in starched white shirts. Jack with his battered whistle, you with your granddad's wheezy old squeeze-box, Willie with his sweet bass voice belting out everybody's favourite airs – while he still had puff in his lungs. The good times.

You fetch the shovel, scrape the rabbits off the tarmac, tip the mess of mashed fur, blood and bones into the wheelie bin, close the gate, look down the road. A big mistake moving into a place where you could still see the pithead and the overhead walkway from your own gate. You should have made a clean break, tried your luck elsewhere. A big mistake but not your biggest, eh Mazzard? The cardboard men are gazing out of the windowed corridor, taking one last look at the day before they descend into the dark, one last glance at the cankered skin of the earth before they slip inside it, before the doors of the cage clang shut and the canaries, in their own cramped enclosures, twitter and fling themselves at the bars.

In spite of the sunshine, you can feel the coming storm in your bones. Your head buzzes like an overloaded fuse box. Your veins sizzle as you stand amidst ox-eye daisies, scruffy willowherb and knee-high grass. In the coop, the canaries twist and turn in panicky loops. It's a diversionary tactic, an attempt to bamboozle a predator with fancy wingwork. Like you, the birds are jangled. Which way to fly? How to escape?

Della won't be diverted. You're old and slow and ache all the time but that's not enough. Nothing's ever enough for Della. She's not far away. On you in no time. No time at all. Soon you will count the seconds between the rumble and the flash. Any time now the first heavy drops will hit your head, you will look up at the sky and see the dark, massed cloud pressing down on the viaduct and, like the canaries, you will panic. You will run inside, bolt the door and leave the coop to mind for itself, let the birds fly madly in every direction, rattling the wire. Though you draw the curtains, turn off the lights, it's not good. A blanket over your head, fingers pressed into your eyes. Willie is still there, his eyes like lamps, following your every movement, never letting you out of his sight. Willie is still there, on the overpass, with the cardboard men, crossing the road forever.

You'll sweat and shiver. Thick ropes of rain will stream down from the pocked stones of the viaduct high above your little house, stream down and lash the roof, walls, windows and doors. Your house sits at the bottom of a rounded valley, a valley like a deep bowl, a chalice set where it will catch whatever comes its way.

The rabbits are in the bin. The coop is locked up. The cardboard men are just cardboard. Replicas, tokens, stand-ins. Nothing more. They have no faces. No features at all. Just pinkish painted ovals beneath cardboard safety helmets. No eyes, no mouths. No bristles push through a shift's deposit of coal dust. No sweat beads on painted brows. No breath stirs in cardboard chests. No songs pour from ruined lungs, no curses either. No curses. But Della will more than make up for that.

You are trying your best to forget, to push it away but the more you try, the more it flies back in your face: those cold dripping walls, the flooded tunnels, Willie wading into an immensity of darkness.

They sang to you. All of you lucky ones. Sang their sweet little songs. Sang their little hearts out. Every one a diva. Every one a twittering star in the dark, a trill of comfort, a match-flame of melody, saving you again and again. And now the redundant descendants of those pit canaries are in your yard, in the fancy coop you tore up your hands building for them. As far as life in a cage goes, they have it good, better than then. Then, those subterranean songbirds had the odds stacked against them.

The sky flares with storm light. Della's at hand. Doesn't come by for nothing. Doesn't like to see things slip, has no truck with time filing down rough edges, bridging gaps, patching up old wounds. Della doesn't go along with forgive and forget, oh no, Mazzard, Della doesn't do forgive and forget. Not her style.

Not just chance, Mazzard, not just chance Della came by. Not just roadkill outside your gate. As you very well know. Nothing accidental about the rabbits.

Around here, around pits, every day's a day of the dead. And this one's Willie's.

Come outside Mazzard. Come out and open up that damned coop. Let those canaries fight it out with Jack O'Lantern's cats. They won't stand a chance but without his wee yellow soprano, neither did Willie. You knew that. Everybody knew that. Come out, Mazzard, go to your gate, look down the road at the cardboard men on the overpass, trudging towards the crumbling, impotent pithead. There's Willie, empty-handed. And you, you're up there too, with Willie's bird swinging on its perch. Let those birds out. Let them sing a requiem, before the heavens open.

Where Even Pasta Breeds

SORRY. SORRY IS how all my sentences seem to begin and most of them never get much further but this is wrong. It's wrong to be so apologetic. Not as if I've done anything terrible. I'd be hard put to say exactly what I have done during the last batch of hours but I get to the end of a day and that's what I'm left with: Sorry. For not being able, more than but maybe nothing to do with, what I am, was, maybe something else, out there. Don't get out there much but out there blows in with its opinions and advice, its good ideas. No end to good ideas. Sorry. That word again. See how I, how I am? I'll make coffee in a minute, soon, if I'm not, if there's no, nothing further, no more *required*. You can be so, you can be up to the elbows in a shitty nappy and the phone rings. You rinse and dry your hands – arms – pick up the baby so it doesn't start *experimenting with texture*, race through the hall with baby jiggling on hip and puking over shoulder on to the only half-decent carpet in the house and grab the phone only to hear some pushy, ingratiating salesperson trying to sell you double glazing, life insurance, a timeshare. If you could take out a premium on time itself, well, yes, I'd sign up for that. But it's always some spiel guaranteed to introduce additional worry into your life: will your windows cave in during the next storm, ruining the furniture, smashing the DVD player, lacerating the sleeping children; will the crack in the ceiling above their beds open up and smother them in rubble? The Brothers Grimm have nothing on telephone sales personnel when it comes to instilling fear. Since the last life insurance call I've been quaking on traffic islands as fire engines and ambulances screech by, convinced that I'm the kind who should have total cover.

The coffee pot is broken. Cracked. I'm out of filters. Tea? I have tea. Is tea okay? Sorry, but I can't see the point of this. I mean, what could I possibly tell you that you don't already know about people like – in my condition. The condition of motherhood. The state I'm in. How could I, this, be called interesting? Do I fit the picture? Am I an example of – incompetence? I thought something might come of this, might become clearer, a way out of, an end but there's no way out, no end, the condition is irreversible, a life sentence. Is there life before death? Do you take milk?

Blessed. You have been blessed. Somebody told me that recently, a childfree woman approaching the age of biological alarm bells, whose eyes ooze droplets of longing every time she passes a pram. We were sitting at my kitchen table. I was in my usual shapeless T-shirt and crumpled joggers. Had I washed my face, brushed my hair? Debatable. I could tell she was concerned about what her clothes might pick up from being in contact with my kitchen table, chairs. But yes, blessed! My hand flew up to slap the blasphemy off her lips but midswing I was distracted. Of course. *Distracted*. I used to like that word. Made me think of oil paintings of girls with creamy skin and heavy-lidded Pre-Raphaelite eyes gazing into the distance. Distance. Space. A clean stretch of hall carpet is my far horizon.

That woman is no longer a friend. She still sends a Christmas card and gifts for the children and calls round from time to time for a quick coffee. Never stays long. *Don't want to keep you back...* From what? I mean, I do appreciate a bit of adult company and beggars can't be choosers. I need it. Whatever's on offer. Whoever. But she's right not to come often. We have no common ground anymore, except the past and Christ, it's taken me long enough to haul myself out of that. Not exactly a holiday, the past.

A holiday. A short break. Yes please. Anywhere. Anytime. I was reading about some outward bound course for young offenders and burnt-out execs. *Maximise your potential. Pit your wits against the elements instead of society.* Reading? That would have been in the health centre waiting room. *Hoods in the Woods*, the scheme was called for the young ones. Hoods, hoodies? I'd say a lot of public money could be saved by letting the hoodie hoods and the execs swap places for a bit. But who'd listen to me? Who'd want to listen to the distracted ramblings of a mother of infants?

My friend, my former friend doesn't. Says she does but she's kidding us both. After a few minutes of nursing her coffee, picking at my unleavened home baking and blowing smoke into the children's faces, a glazed look comes over her face. She sneaks glances at the wall clock, like she's in a hospital and keen for visiting hour to be over, like this condition is only temporary and I'll be past the worst soon. On the mend, back on my feet, out and about, available, game. She talks about her job, her new man, her leisure activities. Leisure! Activities! She's used to beginning a sentence and finishing it but can't do that in my house, or if she does, she finishes it to herself while I'm off seeing to something or somebody. Is this the kind of thing you want? Can you use this?

I don't blame her, really. Means well. Comes up with all kinds of reasonable suggestions. I nod, agree, agree with anything these days because I have so few opinions, thoughts. I do try to think. At night, in bed, I try to plan a strategy for improving on... well, areas for improvement constitute a long list. What happens is, I worry. If the children are sick, I worry. If they're not, I worry about what might happen if they get sick. They're healthy children who, so far, haven't had much wrong with them. I'm lucky, we're lucky, they're lucky but I still worry. About draughts, dust, coughs, allergies, infections. About the crack in the ceiling of their room, break-ins, street fights. And money. Money makes rocks of my pillows.

This morning, like every morning, I tried to keep calm, to keep on keeping calm. I prised the kitchen knife from the wee one's fat, determined fingers while the big one pranced around chanting *gazzibaggitucca gazzibaggitucca gazzibaggitucca*, smirking and jeering, knowing she had something on me, knowing I'd left the knife too near the edge of the counter and something potentially dangerous was happening and she was part of it, knowing I'd been a bad mother for letting it happen, for leaving my children unattended for one minute. One minute! Even mothers need to pee.

I put up with a good ten minutes of the prancing and insane chanting, and the wee one throwing a full-blown puce-faced tantrum, pounding the lino with fists and bootees. I waited. Smiled. Coped. When, eventually, everything was calm again, I began to get the pair of them ready to go out so we could spend some quality time in the park. And then went apeshit over a lost sock.

That was this morning. I don't want to talk about this morning. I don't want to talk about money, the war, things in the house that need fixed – the dripping kitchen tap, the broken toilet handle, the vacuum cleaner buggered by a kirby grip, the living room fire blocked, no what did the gas board call it? Breeched. I thought that meant a back-to-front birth. Or a feet-first birth. What else? There was something else.

My mother phoned. She has bought a hedge trimmer and a shower curtain. My father has taken up asparagus rearing and bringing her breakfast in bed at four a.m. She wanted to know whether her son-in-law would prefer a black or navy pullover for his birthday, which is in three months's time, because the woollen mill is having a sale and she wants to kill two birds. My father is going into hospital to have his toenails seen to.

Yes, I did achieve something today. I got going on one of the kitchen cupboards. It was chock-a-block with stuff. You'd think there was a war on. There is, I know, several wars going on but I can't think about that. Not now. I can think about the kitchen cupboard. Now. I saw the mess, actually noticed it, didn't just shut the door on spilt pyramids of flour, sugar, spices, on gummy smears of jam, ketchup, treacle, on rice grains stuck to soup cans. But it was the pasta shells that really got to me, like clams or snails, some slow-moving infestation. In my cupboard. A place where even pasta breeds.

Fern Heaven

SINCE FERN HEAVEN had gone under, Lilah's husband Sam sat out on the deck a lot, staring at the bay and its traffic of fishing boats, whale watching charters, seaplanes, and the bald eagles which wheeled around on the lookout for scraps. Sam never seemed to tire of the view from their cabin. Though they were up to their necks in debt, the natural beauty of the landscape soothed him, lulled him, let him slump for hours in a bleached wood deck chair, limp as the life-size rag doll in the foyer of the crab bar up the road. When the fern business had been going well, they'd often eaten there. These days, they even avoided walking past.

Lilah had lost interest in living on the waterfront. The planes were noisy and, in season, so were the tourists. Clumps of raggedy kids hung about the wharves, plonking guitars and thumping bongos. The sport fishers and the whale watchers were as bad, yelling news about catches, sightings, tide times and weather forecasts from one dock to another. The noise, the smell of fish which burrowed into the pores of her skin, the salt air which made her hair crisp and tangled as washed-up weed – Lilah could live without the waterfront.

The location had cost them. Their cabin overlooked the sheltered bay but the fern houses, which Sam had built right up by the highway, were close to the ocean. The position of the fern houses had been one of many minor battles between Sam and Lilah, Lilah insisting that a big enough, smart enough sign would tempt most potential customers to pull off the highway and see what lay behind the trees, Sam insisting that out of sight was out of mind. During a storm the previous winter, a freak wave had pounded the coastline, torn up the road, flattened the glasshouses and drowned most everything inside them. Other businesses had suffered damage but Fern Heaven had been the worst hit.

Insurance? Sam, who'd always been good with numbers, would offer lengthy explanations as to why he didn't agree with the premiums, to men like himself who had too much time on their hands. On a good day, Lilah would say to friends: At least we've still got a roof over our heads. On a non-committal day she'd say they'd gotten sick of ferns and their presbyterian fondness for dampness and gloom. On a bad day: Don't even ask. To herself she maintained that if Sam hadn't been so eager for custom, if he'd taken her advice and built behind the fringe of spruce the glasshouses might still be standing. After all, the trees had survived.

One bad day Lilah walked into town and trailed round everywhere she could think of, asking for work, knowing there wasn't any. The season was almost over and nobody was hiring. By the time she went for the bus home, her head ached from smiling too hard.

– And how are you?

– Good, and you?

– Mad as hell. Just passed a bunch of tourists feeding a bear so's they could get in close with their cameras. Criminal. A bear is a wild animal. A fed bear is a dead bear.

Bethany adjusted her baseball cap and started up the little

shuttle bus which zipped back and forth along the coastal highway, picking up and dropping off people wherever they wanted.

– You got no bags so I guess you ain't been shopping.

Bethany had the biggest nose and the loudest voice in town. Habitually, and without malice, she prised people open like clamshells and chucked their innards into the aisle for the edification of whoever was on board. Lilah was glad she was the only passenger. During the ten minute drive back home, unable to offer much resistance to Bethany's sharp probing, she found herself bellyaching about Sam, the loss of Fern Heaven and the unkind act of God which had bankrupted them and dug a trench through their marriage.

Bethany, who had excised the presence of men from her personal life years back, preferring a florid fling with a tourist girl followed by long months of abstinence, was nonetheless a sympathetic listener on the subject, nodding and chipping in every so often with: You're so right, and: Don't I know it. However, Lilah was in no doubt that anybody who didn't already know she blamed Sam for pitching the fern houses in the path of disaster, soon would. Though she took some bitter satisfaction from airing her grievances, Lilah couldn't ignore the cold knot of betrayal twisting and tightening inside her.

When she jumped down from the bus, Sam was in the yard. The trailer of the pickup was already half-filled with chips and shards of the smashed terracotta which had lain in the shed all winter because her husband couldn't bring himself to admit they had no possible use for thousands for broken plant pots. Trekking back and forth with a loaded shovel, his face a mesh of concentration, resignation, failure, he hadn't even noticed the bus stopping, hadn't heard Bethany's yelled farewell. He worked doggedly but clumsily; chips fell off the shovel and trailed a path from the yard to the shed. And this was a man who'd transplanted baby ferns with surgical tweezers.

– Hi. You've been busy.

– Getting loaded up for the dump.

– Good.

Sam's hair fell into his eyes. With a dusty arm, he brushed it back roughly, then coughed, his head hacking into his chest. She hadn't meant to say anything about her conversation with Bethany but seeing him doubled up in front of her, Lilah felt a rush of guilt and pity. And a need to confess she'd been bitching behind his back.

– Guess I betrayed you, hon. Sorry.

Lilah had expected, maybe even wanted some kind of reaction but Sam just pulled on his greying moustache and turned his back on her. Taking her husband's silence to be anger, Lilah, wary and expecting trouble as the day progressed, went indoors. The house was clean and tidy, too damn clean and tidy. Too much time on her hands. Too early to start preparing dinner so she sat at the kitchen table and jotted down possible ways to bring in a few more dollars that didn't involve too much initial outlay – beachcombing, baking for the deli, stringing bead bracelets for the hippies, sewing cuddly whales and bears for the kids. Waste of time. Nickel and dime stuff. Only of interest to tourists. Who wouldn't appear again in large enough numbers until the following season.

That evening, the water was slick and silver as herring. The wooded hills were blue-black. Pale shawls of cloud wrapped around their shoulders. The sky was a deep, clover pink. Lilah padded along the deck, the boards creaking beneath her bare feet. Half of them were rotten. That's what water did; rotted the timbers, not to mention the brain, if you sat and watched it too long.

– Wanna eat soon?

– Hell, yes! Let's have a cook-out, said Sam. It's so beautiful tonight. Salmon, scallops. And wine. Let's have wine.

Sam's enthusiasm startled Lilah. She had become accustomed to him mooching around, listless and uncommunicative, to having a rag doll for a husband.

– Remember what you were saying? When you got off the bus? Been thinking.

– Said I was sorry.

– Whatever. Been thinking and what I been thinking is – I can see a way out for us. An opening. A window of opportunity!

Sam paced around, his hair flopping around his shoulders, grinning like a madman. Maybe he had gone mad. Maybe all that time spent looking at the water really had turned his brain. What window of opportunity could anybody see in betrayal? Unless, unless he meant they should split up. Was that it? They'd come close to it over the loss of Fern Heaven, and a couple of times before that, real close. Was splitting up Sam's idea of a window of opportunity?

– Hey, relax! I'll go pack up what we need. Don't worry about the tab for one night. This is a celebration.

Sam kissed Lilah on the cheek and drove off to town, leaving her dazed, confused and more than a little apprehensive.

Over the food, which after months of pasta and burgers tasted better than anything they'd ever had at the crab bar, Sam expounded his theories about the mathematical nature of betrayal.

– It can be codified. And if it can be codified, it can be put into a programme. That's the beauty of betrayal: a computer can deal with it.

Lilah sipped her wine and mopped up the butter sauce on her plate with a hunk of bread. A pair of bald eagles flew over the roof of the cabin, heading back to roost in a spruce tree. Guitar music drifted over the water. When the sun went down behind the hill, Sam switched on the fairy lights and the deck was bathed in a soft pink glow.

They sat on, oblivious to the biting bugs and the chill in the early fall air. Lilah couldn't think of any reason why Sam shouldn't try to create a computer programme which could write stories – on the theme of betrayal. She wasn't entirely convinced that he was up to it but this wasn't the moment to question her husband's abilities. For the first time since the razing of Fern Heaven, Sam's voice was bright and buoyant.

– The real beauty of the thing is there's not much financial layout. I can do the math, you can help collect some scenarios and once it's up and running, we sit back and wait for hits. Or compose our own bestsellers.

Sam would have stayed out on the deck all night, trawling through technicalities and projecting the possible profit for years to come, if Lilah hadn't persuaded him, in traditional manner, to sleep on it.

Betrayal in all its varieties became, as ferns had once been, Sam and Lilah's obsession.

– It's a causal relationship, Sam said, over a leisurely breakfast the following morning. An equation. Trust then betrayal. Don't work the other way round.

Lilah rubbed her eyes and poured herself a second cup of coffee.

– Say, Sam said eagerly, I tell you I'll meet you at the store at midday then don't show up. If you trust me to keep my word, then I've betrayed you.

– What if you phoned and said you couldn't make it?

– That wouldn't be a deliberate betrayal of trust.

– But say I really wanted to meet you at the store, say I needed to meet you and you cancelled. I might feel let down.

– Let down, sure. Disappointed. Mad, maybe. But not betrayed.

– What if your reason for cancelling was just an excuse?

– Then the situation wasn't based on trust.

– I could have trusted you but you might not have been *trustworthy*. Happens all the time.

– Yeah, but for you to trust me at all, I'd have had to be trustworthy at some point.

– To *seem* trustworthy. Like every Goddamn con merchant around.

– So it's complicated. But I reckon I can make it work. Trust me on this, hon.

Sam took to rising early and spending long hours at the computer, drinking coffee and listening to country and western songs about cheating hearts, lipstick on collars and unfamiliar brands of cigarettes in ashtrays. For relaxation and inspiration, he took his rod and fished off the point; once in a while he brought home something edible. His days began to have a shape to them, a sense of purpose, a momentum. Lilah bought a notebook, a small, ring-bound pad with a pen attached by a silky cord. She began going to town more, to hang out in coffee bars, on the wall outside the co-op or the liquor store, on the wharf where the boats came in. She browsed the shelves of gift shops and the library, ears on stalks.

As well as coming up with scenarios, they needed to find a name for the programme. It was a side issue but still, with millions of sites on the web, they had to have a good name. Sam – who'd been watching some of the Shakespeare productions on Know TV to bone up on some classic examples of betrayal, was keen on Julius Caesar's *Et tu, Brute* but Lilah reckoned the Latin would put people off. They'd seen it with Fern Heaven. Not for the real plant nuts maybe but for the casual fern fanciers, everyday names were more appealing – licorice, leathery grape and maidenhair had the visitors shelling out sooner than *polypodium vulge, botychium multifidum,* or *adiatum pedatum.*

Late one evening, Sam burst into the living room.

– I got it, hon. It's been with us all the time. *Samson and Delilah.*

– Kinda creepy. Just a hop and a skip from our own names.

– It's perfect. A gift. We gotta take advantage of a gift like that.

– Why not *Cain and Abel* if you wanna go biblical?

Sam was adamant that Samson and Delilah was the name

they should go with. No Name Betrayal was Lilah's final contribution of the night. Sam went to bed first, planning an early start to work the next day. Lilah sat on, listening to the soft swish of the water and the putter of a boat's engine in low gear. Samson and Delilah. How did that old story go?

Her grandmother's bible had been sitting untouched in the linen drawer for most of Lilah's married life. The black leather was soft and supple, with a lace of fine wrinkles, like an old hand. Lilah leafed through the gilt-edged pages until she found *Samson's marriage* and *Samson smiteth*. She read from Samson's divinely assisted conception through his slayings and burnings and vengeance wreaked repeatedly on the Philistines, to his spectacular death. The strong man, it turned out, was betrayed by not just one but three women. The first was a nameless woman whom Samson wanted as his wife, the second a nameless harlot. Delilah was third in line.

The first woman wheedled Samson's secret from him on behalf of her people. Because of Samson's subsequent bloody acts of vengeance, she was burnt by those same people. The second woman, the harlot, was again detaining Samson on behalf of her people. Presumably he paid her the going rate, got what he paid for and that was the deal. So not a lot in it for the harlot either. Delilah, though, the bona fide wife, was richly bribed by her people, at a rate of eleven thousand pieces of silver per head, to persuade Samson to reveal the secret of his strength.

Samson held out and held out, eventually gave in to the wiles of the treacherous and greedy woman, was captured, had his eyes gouged out, was incarcerated. While in prison his hair – which Delilah had famously cut off – began to grow again and Samson regained enough strength for a final act of carnage: *the dead which he slew at his death were more than they which he slew in his life*. And that was it for Samson.

But what of Delilah? Did she get the money? Did she avoid the wrath of God? Shouldn't Delilah, as arch betrayer, have had some vengeance wreaked upon her like just about everybody else in the Old Testament? And why did big strong Samson give in to untrustworthy women so easily and so often?

It was daylight by the time Lilah slid into bed beside her sleeping husband, whose hair, fanned out on the pillow, glinted silver as it caught the first rays of sunlight slicing through a chink in the drapes.

Camille

FROM THE BEGINNING I've had to share Camille with countless others but somehow this has never bothered me. In fact, the opposite is true: it adds to her appeal. Observing the intoxicating effect of desire, thirsty eyes drinking in her cool, liquid curves, an impulsive hand reaching out, unable to control the urge to touch, it stirs me too but of course, that's when I intervene. It gives me a mean pleasure, I admit, to stop that hand in its trajectory, to step between it and the object of desire, to have such power over so many rivals. Not that I abuse my power. I am at least superficially sympathetic. I understand the motivation to transgress, to cross the boundary between looking and touching but rules are rules and I am paid to make sure people stick to the rules. They can look all they want, after all, they have paid for the privilege and some would some spend hours salivating over the sleek, small-boned perfection of Camille's body if other interested parties didn't shuffle up behind and nudge them into moving on.

I first became enamoured with my enduring love, my Camille, during a weekend break in Paris. It was spring. The month of April. April in Paris is a cliché of course but after an especially dreich Edinburgh winter I was not at my most imaginative or adventurous. Grey days, I find, numb grey cells. Not that on the weather front Paris was much better. One afternoon was dry enough for the whores to prop themselves in doorways around the Pigalle, bra straps and stocking tops flashing beneath shiny, tightly belted macs but otherwise it rained a lot and when it rains a tourist has no option but to seek out some indoor pursuits. In retrospect, I am immensely grateful for those Parisian downpours. Without them, and without one in particular, I might never have clapped eyes on Camille. Today, Good Friday, I think of as our anniversary.

At first, on the dry days, I took a passing but eager interest in the fabled Parisian whores. Some of them, in their theatrical make-up were stunning and scary, like exotic insects or flesh-eating plants. But even in the youngest, most immaculately presented specimens I could detect the beginnings of decay – a tightness around the mouth, a clouded gaze. And I only had to look along the street at some of their older associates to see how soon life would brown their edges, turn their glossy hair to straw, their porcelain skin to crackle ware.

I did not come to Paris for whores but with the naïve hope that I might meet a girl who would give of herself freely and lasciviously, who would eat me up with her huge French-season-at-the-Filmhouse eyes and spread her endless legs before I'd even thought to ask. But I soon began to wonder just how French women acquired their reputation for sensuality. The ones I met who weren't expecting to be paid by the half hour were ice queens who sneered at my school French and clumsy attempts to chat them up. Couldn't they have been a little kinder to an innocent abroad? Where was their sense of hospitality? Fuck them, was my response after a couple of days of humiliating knockbacks. Fuck them all.

My lack of success made me feel almost nostalgic for Jeanette, my ex girlfriend, who after copious quantities of alcohol, would, on occasion, replace her sober frigidity with drunken passion. One night, in my oppressively dignified pension, contemplating the bidet in my bedroom, I almost called her with the intention of attempting some verbal stimulation. Just as well the cheap cognac I'd been getting through slowly but steadily knocked me out. Jeannette would have perceived my talking dirty as an insult when it was, in my mind at least, a compliment of sorts. But this isn't about Jeannette. And I don't bear her any grudges. One the contrary. By revealing her shortcomings, Jeannette did me a service. I'm grateful to her. She made me appreciate all the more Camille's glowing, immutable perfection.

The trouble with Jeanette and those who preceeded her was quite simple. No matter what had attracted me to any of them in the first place, it didn't last. The face which had looked inviting and alluring in a late night bar, when seen the next morning, creased on my pillow, already betrayed signs of future deterioration. New and startling twists and turns beneath the sheets soon became a wearisome routine. A beguiling personality sooner or later began to irritate. But the worst of it was how deeply unreliable they all were. Not one, in spite of their repertoires of endearing little quirks, made any kind of lasting impression.

I took the job to be near Camille. I moved out of my well-appointed Edinburgh flat, shipped over my belongings and set up in a cramped and squalid little one bedroom apartment in entirely unremarkable *arrondissement*. A surprising amount of Paris is unremarkable. But where I live doesn't matter. Camille will never see the place, or judge me on it. Back in Edinburgh, I used to be quite proud of my flat and kept it tidy and clean enough for most women's taste – changed the bed sheets regularly, cleaned the toilet, did the dishes, attended to the kind of things some of them get nippy about. I provided a good bed, good sofa, some artsy erotica on the walls, a decent sound system. Women felt OK about staying over. One or two, including poor misguided Jeannette, briefly entertained the notion of moving in but I soon put them in the picture. No balled tights under the bed or boxes of tampons decorating my bathroom shelf, thank you very much.

The place I have here stinks of the cats which lurk around the landing doing the kind of thing cats do, the bed creaks hideously, the toilet's only one step up from a hole in the ground but it's all I need. I have no desire to bring anybody home, least of all Camille. Though I doubt she'd give a toss about the state of my accommodation. She's been around, she's a woman of the world, knows the spires and sewers of experience. But if somehow, in another life perhaps, we found ourselves here together, I'm sure that a glass of wine or cognac and a smelly, sexy Gauloise would be all the inducement she'd need to strip off and fuck long into the night.

I have never seen Camille clothed but have concocted many fantasies about what she might wear. Before she takes it off. I've imagined an entire wardrobe for my sweet Camille to divest herself of, just for me. Boots, I think, with thin laces and little heels. A long hip-hugging skirt. A lacy, semi-transparent blouse, high necked, with lots of hooks and eyes, or tiny buttons. And underneath: frilly, crotchless bloomers, stockings – but of course – and one of those whalebone basques. You can't beat a basque: a garment which displays tits and arse at either end like pairs of twin spoons and trusses up the flab in between – whoever invented it was a genius.

My job is not at all well paid, I am obliged to wear a monkey suit and put up with hours of idleness interspersed with idiotic questions day in, day out but I have never once regretted my decision to leave my previous existence and take up a life of servitude on behalf of Camille. To spend my waking hours close to the *déshabillé* body of my beloved is to live each day in a state of bliss. I have no fear that I will lose her, no nagging qualms that any other man or woman might steal her from me. Many others adore her, of that I am certain, but I protect her well from their advances. I'm always alert to someone moving too close to *mon amour*. That is what I am paid for and I love my work. If it were not likely to arouse suspicion, I would do it for free.

A brain is not required, only a keen pair of eyes, a comfortable stance, a few stock phrases in French, German, Italian, Japanese and a firm and vaguely intimidating demeanour at throwing out time. When I think about what my life consisted of before, the effort required to keep on top of my career, the boozing, the shmoozing, the fraught nights spent in pursuit of sexual gratification, I think I must have been mad or just plain stupid. Now, like those dippy hippy types, I have dropped out of the rat race and found happiness in silent contemplation of my ideal. Now the flames of my desire are fed every second of my working day and I am paid for my untrammelled indulgence.

I know every curve of Camille's body, from the nape of her neck to the arch of her foot. I am able to maintain a more or less constant state of mild arousal. Which makes me easy-going and amenable. Which is good for my employers as well as the punters. I am so happy with my situation that I never complain if I am asked to do some little chore not specifically within my remit. In fact, like tonight, on weekends and holidays, I often volunteer to hold the fort, allowing my workmates freedom from the rota to pursue their sad little pastimes. I pity them. They pity me and can't understand why anyone would want to coop themselves up in here when they could be sitting in a café watching *les nanas* on the street or *le foot* on widescreen TV, or traipsing through sodden woods hunting for *champignons*. God, how they bored me last autumn with descriptions of omelettes cooked with chanterelles. At least I keep my pastimes to myself.

There is, of course, security in the building but the directors are very laissez-faire about its deployment. With an elementary grasp of the system and a bit of ingenuity, it's not difficult to find a way of blindfolding the prying eye of a camera. And I do like my time alone with Camille to be private. I can share her for days on end with all those lip-licking oglers but after hours, when I've cleared out the punters, when I've waved goodbye to my workmates as they hurry off, heads filled with their paltry little plans for *le weekend*, when I've bolted the door and set the alarm, she's mine and mine alone.

I draw the thick, heavy curtains, turn the lights off so everything is dark, except for Camille, under a spotlight. Illuminated, she is an embodiment of the sublime: pale and smooth and flawless, stretched out before me in an attitude of glorious, timeless abandon. I undress slowly. I have waited a long time for this moment when we are alone together. Undisturbed. I lean over Camille and press my warm, living flesh against her cool immutable perfection. The initial contrast in temperature, the time and patience it takes to warm her marble breasts in my hands, prolongs my pleasure. I stroke every smooth inch of her, remembering, with a flush of satisfaction, all those other thirsty eyes on her earlier in the day, remember my polite but insistent request: *S'il vous plait, monsieur, ne toucher pas.* I am only jealous of one man: Auguste Rodin, who touched parts of Camille I can never reach.

Jamesie

THE MURDER? UP a bit. Past that lovely laburnum. A bad lot, by the sounds of it. Messing around with minors and what have you. We reap what we sow. Butchered he was. Literally. Joints in freezer bags. Gives a new meaning to the word.

That what's-his-name – chap who writes all the detective stories and is never out of the public eye – they say he's been sniffing around, soaking up the atmosphere. I think we can safely assume that the scene of the crime – and who knows how many others – will feature in some future publication.

I've read all his books. Met him once. At a charity do. Got my photo taken with him. Me all togged up in dicky-bow and DJ. Regular sort of bloke, I thought at the time, if on the scruffy side. But you wonder what effect it has on the psyche, saturating yourself day after day in all that gory detail.

Nice piles up this way. Unless they've been badly chopped up you're talking upwards of a million. Of course the murder will lower the value of the property, though it has to be said, there's bound to be one or two who'd give their eye teeth to buy in to such a chequered history.

Well, this is my stop. Give my regards to your family. Haven't seen your laddies at the pool recently. They should stick in there. A healthy mind in a healthy body and so on. Toodleoo.

People Like Us

SEVENTEEN I MUST have been, or eighteen, a miserable teenager who'd just had her stomach drained after swallowing a bottle of pills, panicking, confessing to a friend, being taxied to accident and emergency. The doctor was rough. The tube down my throat made me retch. It was painful, much more painful than quietly passing away would have been. Being miserable, I wanted sympathy but was given nothing of the kind. When they'd flushed me out and removed the tube, when I'd got my breath back, I told the doctor I thought they could have been a bit more gentle about saving my life. I wasn't sure then that I wanted it to be saved.

He brought his face up close, too close, so I looked away, was looking at his hands when he said:

– We try not to encourage a repeat performance.

He had very male hands, strong and hairy, arched fingers pressing into the bed like tree roots. I was in hideous hospital pyjamas. The top was all askew from writhing and retching and didn't button up properly anyway. My right nipple poked through the striped cotton. Instead of covering it up, I just left it sticking up like a button a few inches from his fingers and wondered vaguely whether, if I rolled on to my side, it would graze against his fingers. But he took his hands away, clapped them together, told me to sleep well, I'd be seeing him in the morning.

I didn't sleep at all. The ward was noisy. The woman across the aisle from me spent much of the night moaning into the darkness:

– They've taken my teeth. I want my teeth. Give me back my teeth!

Eventually the night nurse marched in and flashed her torch around like a cinema usherette until she located the culprit.

– You can't have them. You know you can't so there's no point asking, is there?

– But I feel so humiliated without my teeth.

The woman was left to her humiliation. Like the rest of us in the ward, she'd tried to do herself in and so couldn't be trusted with a set of falsers.

They woke us up at the crack of dawn, poked and prodded and propped us up in preparation for the ward rounds. After tossing and turning all night, listening to snores and murmurs and tears and yells, I didn't feel at all like waking up. But the doctor was coming so I went obediently to the bathroom and washed. No comb, no toothbrush. My mouth tasted scummy and I still looked a mess when I scuffed back to my bed in the awful pyjamas and even more awful slippers – tubigrip bandages knotted at the toes. I looked like I'd been an inmate for years.

I climbed back into bed, shut my eyes and lay waiting for the doctor, *my* doctor, the one whose hairy hands featured in some dazed fantasies throughout the night. I must have dropped off to sleep because the next thing I was aware of was bring shaken by the nurse. Roughly. Rough treatment appeared to be a policy with people like us. I opened my eyes. I had been ambushed. A dozen male medical students and an older consultant – thick eyebrows, thin hair, glinting specs – made a white wall around my bed. Where was my doctor?

Bastard. He'd cheated me. Run out on me.

The consultant pressed bits of me then stepped back to check my notes.

– You were depressed, I understand.

– Mmm.

– Do you get depressed a lot?

– Sometimes. When things go wrong.

– Sometimes. Do you get depressed more then most people?

– I don't know. How much do most people get depressed?

– How much do most people get depressed? Good question.

End of interview but not the end of the scene because nobody was allowed to leave the OD ward until they'd seen the psychiatrist. We had time to kill and hospital time limps along.

– Ah'm no waiting, the woman in the next bed declared. Signin masel oot. Dinnae need a heidshrinker. Naethin wrang wi ma heid. Ah'm no loony. Just cos ah had a few Carlsbergs and a valium cocktail doesnae make me a loony. What else wis there tae dae? Getting turfed oot ma hoose next week. Rent's way behind. Ma man's on a bender. Hasnae been hame for days. The kids are at ma ma's an ah'm rattlin roon an empty hoose wonderin what the fuck's gonnae happen next. Just wanted tae get tae sleep.

The auxiliary wheeled in the trolley and slapped down the breakfast trays on our tables. One slice of hard toast, scraped with margarine and a mean smear of blood-red jam, a child's portion of stale cornflakes floating in too much milk and a mug of tea which tasted like stewed rust. Not much to come back to life for. Not a meal to inspire hope for the future. The woman across the aisle was given her false teeth so she could eat but as soon as the breakfast dishes were cleared away, the night nurse, tired and truculent at the end of her shift, demanded them back.

– I've told you, you can't have them until you've seen the psychiatrist.

I shut my eyes again, tried to block out the woman's renewed protests and concoct a little time-passing fantasy involving last night's doctor. But all that came to mind was the tube down my throat, the retching, the ringing in my ears, the burning in my stomach. And the knowledge that before I got out of here, they intended to flush out my head as well.

I'm a Stranger Here Myself

REALLY. BUT I expect you could tell that from the first time you saw me. New and green, if not so young. I must say, they certainly go out of their way to make you feel comfortable here. I mean, these dressing gowns – bathrobes – made of what's this, velour? – on the outside and terry towelling on the inside. Talk about luxury. The inside mopping up drips and spills, the outside soft and strokable as a baby's head. So soft. Everything's soft in here, the colour of the walls, the curtains – you call them drapes, don't you – the bedspread – do you have another name for that, too? I'm not accustomed to all this softness, to wallpaper which feels like silk, satin pillows which smell of peaches. Even the air feels soft, smooth, blended.

When I walk in here and close the door, it's like being back in the womb, somewhere safe and soft and warm. Not that I actually remember being in the womb but that's the idea I have of it, a warm, pink pool. I talk rubbish sometimes. Do you too? Do you ever say stuff and wonder where on earth the words came from? Like you'd never actually thought something and then you hear yourself saying it, some idea or opinion or theory pops out of your mouth of its own accord? Maybe yes, maybe no? Doesn't matter. You're here. That's what counts.

Know what I do at night when I get back to my room? I unwrap the sweetie the housekeeping girl leaves on my pillow, a glassy lozenge of boiled sugar, fruit flavoured. Lime, guava, cactus fruit, guanabana! So exotic. I suck the sweetie and wander around, my complimentary slippers kissing the carpet. As you can see, I'm a big man. And not known for being light on my feet. But in here I can walk around and make almost no noise at all. Like floating. Maybe it's just that, just this: a room amongst hundreds of other rooms, in the middle of the desert. Seven flights down is a town which doesn't sleep but up here it's just drapes and bathrobes and slippers.

Never see me in slippers at home, either. I'm a stocking soles or bare feet kind of bloke. But here it seems stupid not to try something when it's part of the deal. The romance of it all. A gambling haven in the desert, an all-inclusive price. No, don't tell me. Just don't tell me. I don't want to know. This whole trip is a fantasy. Can we keep it that way? I don't for a minute think you've been waiting all your life for me. I don't think you've been waiting for me at all. It doesn't matter.

I roll the sweetie around my tongue, stroke the furnishings and fantasise about the breakfast buffet. Buffet – it's a banquet. Some nights I've lain awake thinking about what I fancied to eat the next morning. At home my usual's black tea and a bacon roll on the hoof. Here, I've tried all sorts of stuff. Never even seen some of those fruits before. They certainly taste good, though. As long as you know which bits to eat. Made a right fool of myself one morning by trying to eat papaya seeds. Thought they were... I don't know what I thought. One of the other diners asked me if I was trying to grow a tree in my gut. But the breakfasts have been a real treat. And all for the taking. That too. You must know. That more than anything.

So quiet once you get away from all the flash and razzle downstairs. Some nights I've come up in the lift – you say elevator don't you? It sounds more grand, more elegant than *lift* – I've walked down that long dim corridor and not heard a single sound. Weird knowing there are people behind the doors getting up to all sorts but feeling as if you're the only person around when there must be a hundred bedrooms on each floor, a thousand all told. Late at night, it's almost creepy. And if somebody does open a door and comes out into the corridor, I'm not that that keen to pass them. The concealed lighting and the deep hush make it feel more like a set for a TV movie about a hotel than the real thing. And in TV movies, scary stuff happens in dim deserted corridors.

You can tell my imagination runs away with me sometimes. Comes from spending so much time alone. I still like that part of my job: out on the road, nobody breathing down my neck, making my own hours and seeing a bit of the country. A lot of people don't have that freedom. No crap from bosses either, except at pickup and delivery. And no need to join in any workplace banter. If I feel like company, I'll stop for a hitcher or call into one of the transport cafs where I've got to know the proprietors. Not many cafs worth stopping at now, though. The chains as usual have taken over and squeezed out most of the independents.

In here, I keep having to stretch out and touch the walls. And every time I do, I expect them to give if I press just a little bit harder. Not what I'm accustomed to, this softness. I said that already, didn't I? Too much bubbly but what the hell. It's great to be looked after for a change. Not just that. Sitting here, in a luxury dressing gown, on a king-size bed, I feel I could be anybody. Here for the blackjack, maybe, or the poker, or a long, tense session at the roulette table. I could have a couple of Armani suits in the wardrobe – you call that the closet, don't you? That's better too. *Out of the closet* has more of a ring to it than out of the wardrobe. But put me in a setting like this and I feel I could swan down to the gaming rooms and rub shoulders with the rich and famous and beautiful, just the thing. I could play for sky-high stakes and not bat an eyelid when the croupier drags my chips into the bank.

I bet you've seen plenty like me around town, togged up in their gladrags, kidding on for a week or two that this is their natural habitat. I bet you can tell at a glance who's got real money to burn. Truth is, I'm just a slots man. Bit of easy arm action, next to no brain power involved. The barrels spin and I wait for them to settle on cherries or lemons or bells, that's me. And the only suit I own's an ancient thing I shake out for weddings and funerals. Nothing fancy about me at all.

But this place, man. How others live. Sometimes I don't even bother with the slots, I just stop at the bar and watch what's going on. Time to look around has been a real plus about getting away on my own for a bit. Used to go away with a couple of mates, two weeks in Tenerife year in year out. We got on well enough, but both of them are tied up with family now. It hasn't been long enough, though, nowhere near long enough. Especially now. Now I feel like I've just dipped my toe in the water and the tide's on the way out.

Back home? Nowhere like this back home, man. Nothing remotely like it. You could drive the length and breadth of the country and never come across anywhere on anything like the same scale. Usually I stay in during the week. It can be a long day behind the wheel. On a Friday, I'll have a few pints in the pub, talk about the football, the racing, other people's wives and kids, the government. A bit of excess on a Friday is normal. Nothing drastic. Bit of a thick head the next morning. If I'm not working in the morning, I'll have a lie in before I catch up on chores. In the afternoon I might watch the racing. Always an hour or two on the slots on a Saturday evening. It's a quiet sort of buzz, really. Hypnotic it is, the flashing lights, the jingles, the spinning barrels. Sends you into a kind of trance. A pricey trance, yes but relaxing. Soothing.

On a Sunday if the weather's half-way decent I try to get out on the bike for a spin, escape the Sabbath rituals, the hedge trimming and car washing, the gossip at the newsagent's, the refined jollity at the church gates, the teenagers horsing around outside the local caf. On the bike, all I think about is the road and whether to take it at seventy, eighty, ninety. Sometimes I get cocky, think I've got it sussed, that all that matters is me, the bike and the road, everything else is just a hindrance, an obstacle to be overcome. And then I'm leaning into a bend and it comes back to me like a rush of cold air: every corner's like Russian Roulette. One day. One day. And that's why I do it. I know now, going out on the bike has fuck all to do with fresh air and the freedom of the road. It's pitting the wits and staking my shirt against the unknown, hoping to Christ my gut feeling is giving me the right messages.

Here? Well, gambling's the lifeblood of the place isn't it? Can't see why anybody would come here if they didn't fancy a flutter. Though I did see a bunch of Holy Willies out on The Strip one day, distributing leaflets about the wages of sin. Ha! The venues for sin are out of this world. They've thought of everything: the freebies, the ambience, the hot towel massage in the Gents' – the john? – the air conditioning set at the optimum temperature. Everything clean and comfortable and hassle-free. Even still, they can't quite filter out the smell of disappointment. Always hangs around gambling halls, no matter how glitzy they are.

Can't say the slots have been going too well. Don't ask me how much I've lost – nobody ever gives a straight answer to that. Let's just say I haven't quite stayed within my budget. I'm not bothered. This trip has been an eye-opener. Worth every penny. Especially now, up here with you pouring us pink champagne. Pink champagne! Only ever had the stuff at weddings. I hate weddings. Played the sad bastard at the bar too many times.

Hitchers? Mostly I pick up girls. Know they'll be safer with me than with some. But safety isn't what they all want, oh no. Had more than a few of them proposition me over the years and sometimes they got quite shirty when I said I wasn't interested. Took it personally, like my not wanting them to turn a trick was an insult. Even when I told them I didn't think any girl was my type, they weren't always convinced. *You don't look like an arse bandit*, a bolshy little redhead told me. She had a voice like sandpaper. *I can tell an arse bandit a mile off.* Well, she must have needed her eyes checked, mustn't she? Right pissed off at me she was, for wasting her time. Dressed to kill right enough, in the middle of the day, I should have known she was looking for business. But I've never been one to judge a woman by what she wears and if she's got a good body and wants to show it off, so what? I don't see what the big deal is.

Your legs? You've great legs. Really. I've always been a legs man! So long and thin. And in that tiny pink skirt you had on tonight – made me think of a flamingo. *Pretty Flamingo*. Used to dance to that song, way back. Before your time. Before you were born! In the church hall. God, yeah, I danced. On my own mostly. You could do that then. Us lads would do our damnedest to make out it was more cool to dance on our own rather than try for a girl. And run the risk of a knockback.

Your legs were the first thing I noticed. The second was your big feet. No, they're not that big and why would I care what size your feet are? They just made me look again, look properly and work you out. And you caught me looking and stared right back, bold and smouldery. And I knew if I didn't say something, do something, I'd wonder for the rest of my life. Now I'm wondering what took me so long. Yeah, that old sob story. It's not as if I've never thought about it, or never had the opportunity. It's not only girls I pick up on the road and some of the lads make offers too, all sorts of interesting offers. Once or twice I've been tempted. Just never quite taken the plunge. Now? Now I think maybe I've missed out but no sense in going down the road of regret. That's a dead end if ever there was one.

Yeah, the view from the window's amazing. Only thing is you can't see much beyond the main drag because all that neon steeps everything in a tank of light, shuts out the desert darkness. Drowns the stars. Never did get out to the desert. Saw bus trips advertised but didn't fancy trying to take in that immensity of nothingness with forty-nine other gob-smacked tourists. When the tour touts came round the dining room at breakfast and tried to sign me up I kept thinking: that's not the best way to do it. And if I couldn't do it the best way, what was the point? Didn't think I'd get the full effect. Would've hired a bike but I don't have an international licence. Stupid not to have thought of that. Too late now. A bike would have been perfect for getting out there and milking the trip for all that rugged romance.

So I stuck to the slots and mapped out a trip in my head. With you on pillion.

We'd set off late, on the spur of the moment, leave the neon strip behind and head out to the dark, open road. The stars would be very clear and sparkling, a diamante sky. The air would be cool and fresh. We'd drive until we came to an adobe-style motel, with strings of chillies decorating the walls, a billboard advertising a brand of tequila and a sign saying Bikers Welcome. The bar would be quiet and easy-going, a few subdued drinkers in dark booths and a Mexican love song on the juke box. We'd have a couple of tequila slammers, then ask about a room. There would be plenty to choose from and we'd go for one with a big old colonial style bed with a carved headboard and Navajo blankets decorating the walls. We'd strip off our leathers, shower away the dust from the journey, together or separately, then test drive the bed, which wouldn't creak too much at crucial moments. And then we'd dress in clean clothes, I'd be in jeans and a T-shirt – you, I don't know what you'd want to wear in a place like that – we'd go downstairs and eat steak and eggs, washed down with beer, sit around until the barman asked us politely if we needed anything else. We'd climb the stairs and sleep like babies, long and deep until the desert sun woke us the next morning. After a breakfast of ranch-style eggs, I'd fill up the petrol tank – the gas tank? – stock up on cold drinks and we'd head out to the Grand Canyon, to red red stone, blue blue sky, cowboys, medicine men, wild horses and cactus plants and a breathtaking sunset. We'd sleep out maybe, build a campfire, roast something on a spit. Whatever you felt like.

You know, I could get used to these slippers. I could get used to all of this. When I get home, I'll send you a postcard. Of another kind of desert.

See You in Shangri-la

YOU ALWAYS KNEW the time would come for me to say: And now for my last trick. It will, of course be an act with a difference. There will be no smiling sparkling girl at my side, no razzmatazz, no mystified applause, except maybe an echo from Charlie as he swings back and forth on his perch. Don't say: I want to be there. Don't say: You owe it to me, after all I've done. You have been my best girl, of course you have. How else would we have lasted so long? Don't say: What will I do without you? You'll think of something. You always were resourceful. All those costumes conjured from jumble sale rags, all those girlish touches to cheer up a dingy venue, a damp caravan, a tired old trickster like me.

Don't tell me what you're thinking. I know already. It's in your eyes. The tricks are one thing – The Severed Head, The Ethereal Suspension, The Inexhaustible Bottle – but the reality, the frill-free, scary reality of reading minds, which we have shared from the beginning, is a gift no-one should ever take lightly. It has made us quiet around each other, like plants, gently leaning towards the light. Like the Zancigs claimed: *Two minds with but one single thought.* Often it's only Charlie who needs to chatter on. Don't ask me what you should do about him. But maybe hearing him repeat my favourite phrases won't be best for you. Like having an echo of me hanging around, stopping you in your tracks when you need to deal with things. If it was you who was… moving on, I don't think I'd fancy Charlie's rendition of: *Wake up, for God's sake; hang up your jacket; miserable old tightwad* floating around for evermore. Hearing Charlie nagging on your behalf would make me sad.

Not that I want to be forgotten entirely. Just faded to a wispy mist, an essence, an image projected on a cloud of steam, like the boy in the Indian Rope Trick. All down to timing; when to replace the real boy at the top of the rope with the photo projection, when to ease off on the steam, when to switch off the projector and vanish the boy.

You don't have to make any decision about Charlie yet. Wait and see how you feel. Sell him, if you like. Or better still, give him away to a good home. A home anyway. Not the suitcase on wheels we've lived out of so much of the time. A family home with a bit of garden out the back, kids playing on the grass. On fine days his cage could sit outside. Likes the sun does Charlie. Sends him to sleep. Remember that time he fell off his perch and we thought he was a goner when he'd just conked out and lost his grip? Brighton, it was. We were doing a summer run at the pier. A heatwave. Charlie lay on the floor of his cage for an hour while we paced around, snivelling and agonising about whether to call the vet and cancel the show that night. And then he woke up squawking: *Is there a doctor in the house? Charlie is my darling.* Of course you are, old son. My daft blethering darling.

It's the waiting that's the worst. For you too. Not knowing how long it will take to get from this to that, from here to there and what might happen on the way. Another trek to another gig. The packing up, the unpacking and setting up again. All the unforeseen holdups on the way. Some dignity would be a fine thing, some control. Some holding on to the little things as long as possible. Not giving in. Not letting the process get in the way of what matters. And what does matter now, what really matters is that when I'm gone, when this crumbling shell reaches vanishing point, something new and surprising might happen.

This studio's not bad, though, is it? Better than a lot of places we've hung around, waiting to go on, or sat around in after, like tonight, unwinding, taking stock of the show. Feel I should be trying to paint you reclining on the bed, but then again maybe I should be your model. Might find you had a talent for painting. Seriously. We're all full of hidden talents. Often it's just the insignificant little talents that bubble up to the surface, flotsam that's there for the taking, doesn't mean anything. The good stuff's way down. A hidden talent might open up all sorts of opportunities for you. Think about it. Not now. Not if you don't want to. In your own good time. The best transformations require the greatest patience.

We could do the deathbed scene right here. We have the bed, the curtain to be pulled across at the crucial moment. A mock-up. A rehearsal. Like we had for our wedding. A complete run-through of the entire ceremony, just to make sure everybody knew their part. Paid off for the wedding, anyway. Got the parental anxieties out of the way. I don't mean anything, you know I don't. Wouldn't blame any girl's parents for not being over the moon about their only daughter getting hitched to an itinerant magician. Nothing in the way of job security and a string of previous female assistants stretching out behind me. Any parent would see trouble ahead. And behind.

But your folks, to their credit, got most of their gripes over and done with before the ceremony proper and uncle Jack got the chance to call me a Nancy Boy to my face. And live to tell the tale. Me, a Nance – ha! In another life maybe. The long hair, velvet flares – Jack couldn't see past the fashions of the day. Cantankerous old sod but you got what you saw with him. Couldn't be doing with any disparity between appearance and reality. Nobody's fool, if he could help it.

Remember at the wedding proper, when we did The Inexhaustible Bottle for the guests, just before the car arrived to take us off on our honeymoon? Jack had seen a few of the others requesting red wine and beer, watched them drink, amazed, from the same bottle. And then it was his turn and he asked for that malt whisky he loved, Lagavulin. You could see he was wanting to catch us out: wine, beer, gin, vodka, blended whisky – all we'd have needed was half a dozen tubes to swap around. He was sniffing around for an explanation but when he supped from the bottle and tasted Lagavulin, his face was a picture: astonishment, disbelief. Not to mention a large measure of bluster. Almost but not entirely convinced.

After all, he and I'd had a dram or two after the wedding rehearsal, I could have worked out his poison easily enough. It was only after that old buddy of his, Laurence – the one who'd been in the Foreign Legion – asked for and got an obscure country Calvados which was only made in a very particular part of Normandy, that Jack surrendered himself to mystification. It didn't occur to him that we'd find out the favourite tipple of every single wedding guest, or that we'd be able to remember them all. Great, wasn't it? One of the things I've always liked about what we do, what we've done... Nobody has any idea the lengths we'd go to get results. The smart ones believe that if they put their minds to it, they'll be able to cut through the smokescreen. Which is why they're easiest to fool. Ah, well. I suppose I'm no different. Can't keep one step ahead of fate for ever.

So what do you say to a mock-up deathbed scene, a rehearsal – ha! Tacky, sick but that way you'd get the speech I'd like to make, a proper, planned one in which I told you all the things I've never got around to mentioning – stuff saved for a rainy day on some weatherbeaten site somewhere, the wind rocking the van from side to side, the windows dripping outside and in, a cold blast slithering under the door. At some point most people must have a go at composing their own deathbed speech. Pity so few ever get a decent airing.

Are you up for it, to being entrusted with my innermost thoughts? You must know most of them already: my hopes and fears, my moments of pride and shame but maybe things still need to be voiced so there's no doubt, no misunderstanding. Words change when they're said aloud, when they're thrown into the open. It's a trick of the voice, a kind of ventriloquism. Words can be ugly or cruel but while they nest in the head, private and unspoken, there's always some charm, some appeal, something innocently seductive about them. They can incubate with... impunity. Impunity – ha! *Nemo me impune lacessit.* Remember when that squaddie guarding Edinburgh Castle translated the Latin for us: *wha daur mess wi me.* Ancient Order of the Thistle, he said. You taught him a cup-and-balls trick he could have found on a cereal packet and he let us in to see the Stone of Destiny for free. Which wasn't much to look at, considering all the hoohah about it, a dull lump of rock. Maybe that's what destiny always is in the end. But there. Eventually. No matter what. Sorry, rambling.

Don't feel bad. And don't worry. No nasty surprises up my sleeve. No birds dead or alive, no phantom arms. Phantom arms, ha! Funny to think of that now. Forget the bed. Plenty time for beds. I'll stand, with Charlie on my good arm. I can see you better, sitting on the artist's chair set behind the easel, the milky light from the window pouring over your back. I can see so much more now. The girl you were, the woman you've become, so many transformations illuminated one by one as you turn your head. Stop me if I get too mawkish.

We could do with a few tricks of the trade right now. A few more illusions. You and I have got by on illusions. And maybe because we know how illusions are made, we can't fool each other. Or ourselves. Which is as it should be. But a bit of razzmatazz wouldn't go amiss, some *legerdemain,* some *prestidigitation.* Lights, costumes, some *phantasmagoria* to lift the atmosphere, get the show off the ground. I feel I'm missing something, as if I've lost my props. Like that time we left Charlie's cage on the train. Wales, it was. The van was at the garage again. Buggered suspension, the usual. Not surprising, considering the way we loaded the old thing down with our entire lives. Trying to transport all that stuff by train was madness but we never could risk turning down a booking so there we were, unloading packing cases at Rhyl – changing trains for Bangor, was it? – when the train moved off with Charlie still on it. All the way to Aberystwyth and back he went. Not that he was any the worse for his escapade. Picked up a couple of Welsh swear words en route and tickled the audience good style. On great form that night. Tonight too, my old son. You've done us proud.

Should I smile? Or stay straight-faced? I feel I should be smiling, ruefully – is that the word? No matter. Smiling all the same. After all, I'm a believer. If we could convince people to suspend their rational minds and believe, for the duration of the act that I was packing you into a box and sawing you into pieces – with or without blood – who's to say there's not a truly mystifying illusion someplace else? An earthly paradise above the clouds. Lost Horizon. Shangri-la. A place where a person can live as if they were forever young. And the great thing is, getting there isn't sudden or terrible, just a dreamy kind of slowing down, like you get in a crash, that mesmerising parabola looming up and sucking you into its long slow curve towards the inevitable wall.

Preparation is all. With the right preparation almost any kind of illusion can be pulled off. And I've been preparing. I've been holding my breath for as long as possible, memorising every expression on your face, every twitch of Charlie's beak, every ruffle of his feathers. I'm ready. Nearly, except that I keep thinking somebody somewhere has set me up. Remember that story about Houdini, when the cop buggered up the handcuffs they used to restrain him? Houdini could pick any working lock and one locksmith to another was fair game. But a faulty lock, a faulty lock was cheating. Not that I'd ever think of comparing myself to the greats but I keep thinking there's a catch somewhere, that everything will move along smoothly and then, hey presto, lead shot in the works. A trick is one thing. Cheating can kill – Ha!

Don't say it. I know. Don't toss the words into the air, like doves or hankies or coins. Don't make me drink from the inexhaustible bottle of regret. Let it go. Let me go. I'm ready. Nearly. If I had some spectacular confession or secret disgrace, some painful but still poignant and meaningful incident to disclose – something to tell you that you don't already know, something big and important to leave you with... I'm not saying I don't have secrets, everybody does, but the truth is mine are ordinary secrets. I have nothing to amaze you with, hidden up my sleeve. Still, now's the time to open up my box of tricks, display it from every angle so you'll see I've nothing to hide.

Here I go. Are you sitting comfortably? This is about cheating pure and simple. Me, cheating. Maybe you already know, or have already guessed, there's so little you don't know about me, or haven't worked out. So little. Living in each other's pockets all these years, there's plenty time to scrutinise the contents but there's just one thing I want to tell you about. It goes back a bit. To just before our first meeting.

You were working in the cloakroom of that club – the Riviera – down by the docks. Strippers on Friday nights and variety acts on the Saturday; singers, dancers, comics, magicians. No child prodigies. It wasn't a family show. My assistant then was a girl called Colleen. Irish, yes. We'd had an act going for a couple of years and a romance for about the same time. A grafter was Colleen, with dark good looks, a hot temper and a vast collection of high-heels. We rubbed along pretty well. Only problem was that she'd begun to get very keen to tie the knot, make us official. Which was the last thing I wanted. Then. It was coming up to her birthday – all of twenty-five she must have been, and she wanted an answer. If I said no, I'd lose her, if I said yes... I didn't want to say yes.

Our dressing rooms were not, as we'd requested, next to each other: mine was near the main door where people were coming and going all the time, Colleen's was down the corridor. I was happy enough about the distance. As I said, strippers had been on the night before and had used the dressing rooms. I was in my costume and was bending down to tie my shoe laces when I noticed a pair of knickers under the dressing table. The cleaners must have missed them. Silky pink with black lace trim. Fancy pants, as me old mum would have said. They'd been worn but only briefly. And no, I didn't make a close inspection. The kind put on to be taken off. Trimmings for late night nookie.

Maybe the girl had private customers, maybe her boyfriend was waiting for her at the end of the show, who knows. I wondered if she always carried spare underwear in her handbag or if she'd gone home knickerless, letting the cold wind whistle up between her legs – sorry, sorry. Of course I didn't fancy the stripper, I never met her. Anyway, I was feeling a bit hassled by Colleen, the pressure to conform, to keep her parents happy, make an honest women out of her – all the usual stuff people agonised about then. I strung the knickers across the top of the mirror between two hooks, began to put on my make-up. As always, Colleen came to my room shortly before we were due on, to run through some last-minute details about the show. And to peer over my shoulder into the dressing-table mirror to check my make-up. Never had much faith in my ability with an eyeliner pencil. The first thing she saw was – you've got it. I could have explained the knickers away in a minute – even if

I couldn't quite explain why I'd chosen to drape them across my mirror. Still not sure about that. Not as if I had a thing about women's underwear, I mean, nothing out of the ordinary. But I said and did nothing to put Colleen's mind at rest. I just continued applying my eyeliner as she turned her gobsmacked gaze from the knickers to me.

– Tell me they're not yours, she said, very slowly.

I had to laugh. She and uncle Jack would have made a right pair, wouldn't they?

– They're not mine, I said.

– Then whose are they?

The five minute light bleeped in the dressing room. Perfect timing. I unhooked the knickers, folded them up and put them in the drawer.

– We'll talk after the show, I said.

– Too right we will.

At that time I was just beginning to develop the skill of thinking about two things at once. All through our act – a warmup for a foul-mouthed comic – as we went through the show, which included a couple of new pieces we were still perfecting, part of my brain concentrated on what I was doing and how the audience was responding, the other part considered Colleen and the rest of my life. And, somewhere around the middle of the finale, a crowd-pleaser with ribbons and doves and Colleen doing cartwheels, I came to a conclusion.

Straight after the show, as soon as we were back in my dressing room and the door was pulled, she was onto me about the ownership of the knickers. I had already decided what I would say.

– They belong to the girl in the cloakroom.

Yes. I said they belonged to you. Sorry. And what's worse is, at that moment any cloakroom girl would have done. So at the end of the night, when I came up and handed over the knickers and asked for them to be put in lost property and you, discreetly, slipped them under the counter, and I chatted you up whirlwind style and asked you out, it wouldn't really have mattered whether you'd said yes or told me to piss off. Colleen saw me speaking to you as if I knew you, she saw me putting my hand on your shoulder. Colleen, who'd assisted me in countless illusions, fell hook, line and sinker for the cheap trick I played on her.

So there it is. Sorry Colleen. And sorry you. Even from before we met you have been my accomplice – unwittingly at first, unwillingly later, I'll hazard a guess. And now, now it's time for you to take matters into your own capable hands. And make me vanish.

Toybox

AS ELLEN AND Sumona drag the tea chest into the middle of the floor, the girls from the convent school troop past the window, dazzling in white frocks, white ribbons which secure glossy black braids and white ankle socks turned neatly above sturdy lace-up shoes. The sweet scent of coconut hair oil lingers in the wake of the ordered line of well-fed, well-dressed, well-behaved girls. Little angels? Privileged brats? They are still young, these girls, no more than eight or nine but at home some of them are already giving orders to the servants, already comparing their smooth, honey-coloured skin to the burnt-stick colours of housegirl, cook, gardener.

– Did you play with dolls, Sumona?

– Of course. Dressing and undressing. Mummies and Daddies. Doctors and nurses. You?

– I cast them as characters in stories. Fairy tales. Cinderella was a favourite.

– We also have a version of that story. Rags to riches. A universal dream.

Drawing the curtain across the mosquito mesh, to cool down

the room and afford their own children some respite from the sidelong glances and barely suppressed titters of the convent girls – Ellen catches sight of the last of them, skipping to catch up with her class as it files past a tall, straight-backed nun and in through the reinforced school gates with their embellishment of broken glass along the top. A beautiful girl, with flashing eyes and perfect teeth, Ellen recognises her as the daughter of Mr P, as everybody calls the small coastal town's only lawyer.

Mr P is a busy, important man. Every day of the week, outside his dazzling white house, a queue of wilting clients can be seen waiting under the merciless glare of the sun. There are no benches to sit on. Only a wall to press against in the hope of catching a thin wedge of shade under the roof. The clients wait, often for hours, in the hope of gaining an audience with the lawyer. Sometimes they are successful, sometimes not. In seeing him, if nothing else. Sometimes they go home at dusk and return again the following morning. Mr P doesn't operate an appointments system. He doesn't need to.

In the afternoons, when there is no school, his daughter sits in the dappled shade of a banana palm and swings to and fro on the creaking garden seat. She plays with toys and sips lemonade brought on her own shrill orders by the housegirl. Who is, of course, a grown woman in an ungrown, poorly nourished body.

When Ellen went to ask Mr P's advice, she was immediately ushered into his pink, fan-cooled office. He would hear none of her protests about jumping the queue.

– I couldn't possibly leave a British lady with such delicate skin out there. I would not forgive myself. Our sun is very violent, you know. You would fry in a minute, my dear lady.

He offered a choice of refreshments: whisky, gin and tonic, Coca-Cola, iced tea, opened the door to his office and barked Ellen's request down the hall. He remained standing, lifting a slat of the pink venetian blinds with his pinkie.

– These people, he continued, his voice instantly reverting

to the mellifluous, They are used to the heat. They are acclimatised to it. And to waiting. Everybody knows I pride myself on thoroughness, on taking my time, which I'm sure you will appreciate is an essential quality for making correct decisions. If a job's worth doing and all that. And a job cannot be done well without all the relevant facts at one's disposal.

The housegirl, stooped as an old woman, hurried in with a glass of iced tea on a tray. She set it down in front of Ellen.

– Don't shake the table, girl, snapped Mr P.

The housegirl stooped even lower, hurried out of the room.

– Now, he said, sweet-voiced once more, Tell me why you are here.

The man's ability to alter his tone of voice so radically – from barbed wire to honey and back to barbed wire – had a vaudeville quality to it, reminding Ellen of puppet booths set up on a beach or esplanade in the summers of her childhood. One person would do the voices for all the puppets, exaggerating their differences for dramatic effect. Of course, there was only room for one person at a time in the tiny, striped booths but as a child it was a discovery which had made her feel cheated somehow, duped. As she did now. As if Mr P didn't know why she was there. Ellen had explained – again – that it was impossible for her to provide all the facts about children whose parents had been removed, disappeared, eliminated under a spectrum of unclear but unquestionably brutal circumstances. Mr P stuck to his guns. Politely but firmly, smiling broadly, sympathising effusively. Refusing, graciously, to help.

The gate is bolted behind the dazzling convent girls. The school bell clangs. Ellen and Sumona invite their children to come close, sit down. It takes a while, as it always does, to persuade them to abandon their solitary lookout posts dotted around the extremities of the room, to come forward and form a ragged circle around the tea chest. One by one, the children take a few steps forward but they are hesitant, tense, ready to retreat in an instant to the edge of the room, as if they're playing a sort of back-to-front Grandmother's footsteps and the objective is to be last to reach the tea chest. The new boy stays in his corner. Which is only to be expected.

Once the more well-adjusted children have crept forward and squatted down, Sumona tells them about the chest:

– This may look like an ordinary tea chest, children, but it's not. It's a treasure chest. Inside are all kinds of surprises. Nice surprises. For all of us to share.

The chest is stamped with the name of the convent: *Little Sisters of Fervent Hope*. It is thanks to the nuns' commitment to charity that these dead-eyed children, who wake in the night screaming and tearing at themselves, who whisper and creep by day are here at all, with clean water, food, a roof over their heads. And now even toys to play with. Ellen and Sumona call them *their* children because they are, now, nobody else's.

Sumona yawns, rubs her eyes which are dark-ringed from lack of sleep. Ellen's head throbs from the heat and weariness. The two women try to take turns of night duty but more often than not, both are needed to cope with night terrors. Even here, in what is for the time being at least, a safe place, darkness gives shape and voice and substance to real and imagined demons. Last night the new boy, whom Sumona has named Sumatibale after her own lost brother, kept both women up most of the night, singing lullabies, trying to hold him steady, safe while he rocked and raved. Now he is crouched in the far corner of the room, gnawing the skin off his fingers.

One by one, Ellen takes the toys out of the chest. As she spreads them out on the floor, Sumona, with as much enthusiasm as she can muster, states what they are. A few of the children repeat the names listlessly as bricks, trucks and Barbie dolls appear in front of them. Others simply stare. One or two creep a little nearer. But not too close. Their children never come too close. And their eyes remain trained on Ellen's hands as if she might pull something terrible from the toybox.

Not one child tries to grab a toy. Sumona explains that the toybox is a gift from the convent, that the toys are for fun, for playing with. Even then, no child reaches out a hand. In spite of the sun already beginning to warm the room, Ellen shivers. Once she would have been amazed, even appalled at the idea of having to teach children to play. Not now. Not much amazes her now. And perhaps, too, less and less appals her.

There are more Barbies than anything else and all except one, modelled on Naomi Campbell, are California blondes. The solitary male doll is a miniature, square-jawed American hunk, in jeans, check shirt and baseball cap. At least he's not in combat gear.

– Haven't the Sisters been kind, says Sumona. All these presents! All these toys! We can have lots of fun! So many games to play!

Of the other dolls, some are kitted out in lurex and electric pink disco gear, black and gold ball gowns, wedding dresses and veils. Some, in homemade clothes, have had their locks shorn by convent girls playing at hairdressers. Some are naked. A few are missing limbs. Ellen had hesitated about bringing out mutilated dolls but, after all, several of their children have scorched, maimed or missing limbs.

Ellen smiles at the children, as she tries to do as often as possible, even though they hardly ever smile back. Picking up a doll which has been dressed in a homemade nylon sari, she demonstrates how the arms and legs can be moved as if the doll is walking, or the head turned from side to side as if she is looking over her shoulder at somebody:

– At a friend, Ellen says. She's looking at a friend.

She goes on to show how, like a real one, the sari can be unwound and retied in different styles. As she is attempting to secure the slippery cloth around the doll's shoulders, the head loosens, falls off, drops into her lap and rolls on to the floor. The new boy screams and sobs and batters his own head against the floor. The others back off slowly, staring in horror and confusion as Ellen hurriedly attempts to reunite the doll's body with its head.

– It's OK, she says, smiling so hard that her jaw hurts. I can fix her. I can fix her.

Warily Sumona approaches the new boy, clasps him gently in her arms, feels his hot tears soaking through the thin cloth of her sari. She remembers her brother's horror at finding a headless bird which the cat had left at the door, her own at coming upon a monitor lizard on the beach, eating a dead dog. Ordinary, everyday horrors. Slowly, softly, she explains to the boy that the doll has been handled roughly in the past, as he has, but if it's treated gently now, it will be fine. And so might he. In time.

– Look! says Ellen, in the bright, brisk peal of a steely nurse. All better!

She has managed to twist the Barbie's head back on to its neck and transform the sari cloth into swaddling. Now she cradles the angular plastic body in the crook of one arm. Rocking it gently, she begins to sing a lullaby:

– *Hush little baby, don't say a word, mamma's gonna buy you a mockingbird…*

Remembering how the song continues, that litany of unlikely gifts, Ellen gives up on it. One of the girls, Nadia, gets the idea. With the care and delicacy one might give to an injured butterfly she picks up another Barbie, shorn like herself, in a homemade dress, and holds it to her chest.

The new boy is still gulping and sobbing but allows Sumona to stroke his head. Ellen tries to interest him in a battered green truck.

– Brrmmm, brrmmm! Brrmmm, brrmmm!

She demonstrates how the wheels turn then gives the truck a push so it runs a short way across the concrete floor. The boy peers out from under Sumona's arms. Ellen repeats the procedure. The boy's too-large eyes follow the truck's movements and remain fixed on it when it comes to a stop, as if expecting something else to happen.

– You can try it if you like, says Ellen.

The boy looks away.

– Whenever you want.

Turning her attention back to the other children, Ellen begins to build a rudimentary house from bricks. Inside the protective walls she places the Barbie with the detachable head. Nadia copies her, glancing up shyly for approval.

– Good, Nadia. There's still room in the house for more. And we can make the house bigger if we want. Look everybody. We can use more bricks and build an extension so none of the dolls needs to be left out. Would anybody else like to help? When we do something together it doesn't take so long.

As another child tentatively moves towards the toys, as things appear to be improving a little, Sumatibale punches his way out of Sumona's grasp, grabs the truck and slithers across the floor, dragging his crushed leg behind him. With deadly precision he sets down the truck and wheels it over a convoy of ants which is crossing the floor in a thin, purposeful line. His eyes are glassy with concentration as he then wheels the truck backwards, squashing those which survived his first assault. When he's convinced that he has halted their progress, that the ants are either dying or already dead, he slithers back to his corner, muttering.

As usual, the other children don't respond. Rarely do they respond to anything, as if they want nothing more than to shrink into themselves, become invisible. Don't react, don't ask questions, don't draw attention to yourself. A strategy for survival, this shrinking, and survival is what all of their children know best. Pleasure, play, these are luxuries. Healing takes time and Ellen and Sumona don't know how much time they will have to ease off the burning, choking, scratching necklaces of fear which encircle their children.

– We'd better have a look at this morning's drawings, she says. The report is due soon. The progress report, which might send some of them back to what they escaped from. If enough progress has been made. To Ellen and Sumona rehabilitation has become a dirty word. As has progress.

– What do we say this time?

– God knows. We have to say something.

Neither wants to look at the drawings. They know what they will contain: guileless depictions of atrocities – drawn from life. But in order to offer any of their children even temporary respite, in order for the generosity of the convent to continue, they have to complete the report.

As the sun climbs higher in the sky and the temperature inside rises sharply, the smell of the nearby market seeps into the room, rank and sour, a smell of bruised, fly-blown fruit, fish guts, blood. It rained mid-morning, a brief, heavy downpour which for an hour or so turned the streets to muddy rivers. The townspeople splashed by, heads covered with umbrellas or banana leaves, unconcerned about the incongruity of keeping your head dry while you were ankle-deep in mud.

The day before, they'd taken their children to the market. An experimental outing. They went first thing in the morning, before it became too busy and the bustle might have been overwhelming. The streets were dry and dusty, the fruit on the stands ripe and luscious. Sumona asked one of the vendors to split a pineapple between them. Ellen passed it around. Suspiciously, the children held up segments of bright fruit like the smiles which so rarely graced their faces. They had to be persuaded to eat quickly, before the flies descended. At first the vendor had been impatient at their reticence, lack of appetite, but when Sumona explained where they came from and where they might be sent back to, if Mr P in his pink office continued to insist on having all the facts at his disposal, he split them another pineapple free of charge.

The school bell clangs once more, flat and heavy, shuddering through the room. Soon after the bell, the shrill voices of the convent girls, the splashing of their sturdy shoes on the muddy street as they hurry through the gates, keen to get home to lunch cooked by the housegirl, and an afternoon's amusement in a shady garden. The convent girls flock past the window, darting shadows against the drawn curtain. Inside, in the blistering heat, Ellen and Sumona's children stare numbly at the hardly-touched array of toys. Snuffling and whimpering, the new boy once more crawls out of his corner. With a bloody fingertip, he tries to set the squashed ants back on their feet, coaxing gently, pleading with the crushed carcasses to rise from the dead and walk.

Gilbert

ISN'T HE BEAUTIFUL? Don't you love that charcoal curve from
the buttock to the back of the knee? Can one ever have too
many nudes? What do you think Bacon was up to, painting all
those Popes? Don't you think a limner is closer to God than
anyone? Did you like my favourite waiter? Would you care to
listen to some Bach? Preludes or fugues? Does it matter at all
that we missed the party? Should I open another bottle? Red
or white? Do you have to smoke? Weren't you just a little
relieved? Shall we take our drinks out to the roof garden? Are
you warm enough? Should I fetch blankets? Is my ficus poorly?
Were you sure he'd show up? Isn't this the best view in the
city? What time is your train? Do you require breakfast? Will
you be miserable tomorrow? Didn't we have a good time?

Yves

THE FRENCH EXISTENTIALIST has left the locale, abandoned his diet of days at the library, his ponderous, thought-laden strolls. He no longer stops to enquire about the sex life of neighbourhood cats; no longer contemplates the sinuous ramblings of clematis, the disintegrating fence; no longer, at inordinate length, considers turnip, beetroot, okra, the dark-eyed boredom of the greengrocer's daughter; no longer stands in the dark, constructing hypothetical definitions of lives in lit windows; no longer postulates a theory about why encounters with blossom, leaves, mud, snow don't make him feel more at home.

The French existentialist has returned to Lille, Lyons, Lavigny. A faint smell of anise hangs in his cluttered, dusty room. Daily, he takes his thoughts to the river, the lake, the canal. He pulls them from his pocket, his crumpled thoughts, throws them in the air and waits for them to settle amidst familiar blossom, leaves, mud, snow.

The Grand Canal

CLAUDIA AND PAOLO have lost their way and wandered far from the glittering honeycomb of shops selling glassware, leather, masks for Carnivale, far from the gondolieri, crumbling palazzos, and the mingled odours of coffee, garlic, pastries and perfume. In the dank tangle of backstreets where doors are barred early against the night and only cats skulk and fuck in the dripping shadows, Paolo says:

– Everybody gets lost here. It's part of the fun.

He closes in on Claudia, nuzzling her neck so she can hear his breath and feel the heat of it. He nudges her against the flaking wall and probes her clothes for gaps, skin.

– Alone. At last.

–You're crazy.

– For you.

– OK so they don't have cars here but it's still the street, Paolo... and we're so late.

– I can live without those guys a bit longer.

– We must be near, I mean, I can hear the vaporettos. You only get them on the main drag. Can't you hear the vaporettos?

– Relax. Jeez, can't you ever relax? We're a long way from Little Italy. Nobody's grandma's up at the window spying and saying novenas.

– I don't want this, says Claudia, pushing him away.

– Me neither, babe. Me neither.

Paulo marches off. Claudia follows, a few steps behind. As Paulo turns yet another blind corner, his arms fly up as if the scene had been thrown at him. Beneath a garland of coloured lights the black churning waters of the Grand Canal - which they have been trying to find and missing for one long quarrelsome hour – are now in front of them.

– Happy now? he says.

Claudia stops, hoping that Paulo will come back for her but already he is waving to someone he sees further along the footpath.

When she reaches the open door of the tile and chrome place where they had arranged to meet the others, Claudia stays outside. Paulo has already been drawn into the throng of students crushed around the spurting espresso machine, into the loud, careless exchange of greetings, jokes, backslaps and kisses. Claudia leans against the outside wall, hands behind her back, fingernails digging into spongy, pitted stone. She wants the view to wash over her; the boats, lights, water, wants to be rocking across the canal in a gondola with Paulo, the romantic tourist thing.

– Gondolas are a total rip-off, he told her, when she pointed hopefully at a slinky, black boat. Soon as these guys hear American they treble the rate and take you the long way round. Couldn't she see they'd be blowing the last of their Euros on something totally phoney? And what was so great, Paulo had wanted to know, about being punted down canals by some surly, sweaty boatman in fancy dress, who'd reek of garlic and look up her skirt? Wasn't wandering around, finding their own way more fun? Well, no, it hadn't been fun at all.

It's the last night of the study tour. Claudia couldn't care less about the party but can't shut out the sound of everybody else having a good time. Laughter pours through the open doors of the cafe and in spite of herself she sneaks a look inside. Fllamma and Anna are leaning against the bar, holding up souvenirs haggled over on the Rialto; miniature Davids dangle from key-rings, rise out of ashtrays, scowl down from T-shirts. The thing about The David is how pissed off he looks, as if he'd known what the future would do to him; reproduce him by the million, shrink him, turn him into a cheap joke.

Ricci and Tosca are watching the scoreboard flash and spin as Julio thumps the flippers of the pinball machine. Gianna and Maria sit nearby on high stools, absently stirring Campari sodas. Whenever either of the guys at the pinball table glances away from Julio's rocketing score the girls turn their heads a fraction. The others are bunched together. Claudia sees a glinting neck chain, a tossed-back lock of hair, a finger wiggling into an ear, an arm hooking another, the moist, besotted eyes of Georgio, the slim pink tongue of Pucci flicking across her lips as she inclines her great bone structure to Paolo.

For the crowd in general and Pucci in particular, Paolo is all smiles yet since the first wrong turning tonight he's been a misery and a moan. And he must have known Claudia couldn't turn on just like that, in the frigging street, just because it suddenly occurred to him, just because they were on their own. For once. She'd wanted to be alone with Paolo, too, she'd been aching for it, to wander around, just the two of them. In theory, getting lost had sounded pretty cool but he'd gotten all fired up on grappa before he met her, was rough and clumsy and his kisses tasted bitter. Now Claudia wants to spit out the taste of Paulo.

He wasn't good looking – and when he was angry, his heavy brow and slack mouth looked dumb, bullish, but the guy always knew how to have a good time and normally where to find it. Even here, in Venice, it was Paolo who'd found the best places to go, Paolo who'd charmed the crabbiest waiter into finding a table for a big wild bunch of kids. Paolo who'd stood up to Crolla. That morning the professor had raged at Pucci for appearing at the breakfast table in her bathrobe.

– You want her to take it off? Paulo asked the professor, cool as they come.

Pucci crossed her legs, letting her robe slip off her silky tan thighs. That was the start of the old guy's rant about the crassness and vanity of youth which continued all the way to the Lido.

The day was sticky and overcast, a heat haze turning the distant city into a silvery scribble of itself. Crolla had brought the class to the beach to discuss its appeal to painters and filmmakers and was boring everybody rigid with an excess of technical stuff about light and shade when all they wanted was to chill.

– We'd learn more about this shit by drawing some of those cute beach bums, Pucci said, and wandered off to the water's edge.

Crolla's cheeks purpled, his eyes went thundery.

– Say goodbye to your credits, he said, in a raging whisper.

Pucci couldn't care less about credits. College was just somewhere to hang out for a while and art history had looked like a soft option. Pucci had no interest in the glories of Venice. She stalked the narrow alleyways, all angles, arrogance and invitation though rarely responded to anything except designer accessories and her own reflection in storefront windows. And being with the class bored her more than anything; Pucci didn't deal with college kids. Except Paolo maybe. On the Lido, Claudia can't help remembering, only Paolo had been honoured with Pucci's golden, slant-eyed pout.

It is Georgio who brings Claudia an Orangina and stays beside her, shifting from one big foot to another, Georgio who lingers, disturbing Claudia's stubborn silence with bursts of rapid, nervous chatter. He's really got a lot from the study tour, the galleries and churches. Isn't it something to see so much culture in one small city? It really makes him feel proud to be related to it all, even if nobody back home gives a shit about anything but real estate. This city of lovers has cast its spell on him. He wishes he wasn't but he has to admit that he's seriously in love with Pucci, he's not just after her ass like everybody else. Pucci's not what she seems, no, she's a shielder, nobody could be so Goddamn closed off for no reason. Giorgio knows Pucci doesn't even see him never mind think about him but some day she'll need to talk, everybody does, and when that happens, he plans to be there for her. Claudia reckons Georgio should give up liberal studies and go into seminary school.

– Go back to the party, Georgio, says Claudia. I don't feel like company right now.

But Georgio says no, he can see she's got problems, maybe she should talk about them. Or not. Either way's OK with him. Although Georgio is doing his best to make her feel better and sincerity oozes from his deep, gloomy eyes, Claudia is still mad she's not with Paulo, that things aren't working out and being Paolo's girl is not so great but it's getting cool out, too cool for the vest and miniskirt she wore because Paulo liked to see her legs. On Georgio's arm she could slip inside and speak with whoever until she found herself next to Paolo and it would just happen, a word, a hug and everything would be just fine again. No scene. She hates scenes.

– Hey, babe, what's up? You wanna do it with him when you can have me?

A bunch of kids bursts on to the terrazzo, Paolo up front, grinning like an idiot as he's propelled towards Claudia. His hands clamp her waist, thumbs hook beneath her ribs. He picks her up, throws her in the air and just before her feet hit the ground pulls her into a clinch. The others whoop, whistle and clap and it's worse, much worse than being ignored, Paolo reclaiming her like this with the whole frigging class gawping at them, turning them into a street show. Clutching her like a piece of baggage, dragging her across the cobbles in a drunken stagger and the class is too busy cheering, too taken up with the spectacle, too busy being entertained to notice them veer too close to the edge, lurch off-balance and plummet into the swaying murk of the Grand Canal.

The dark, cool silence, the absence of everybody and everything but her own body, sinking... but shit she's in the filthy frigging canal and her lungs are deflating like spent balloons.

When she surfaces, the first thing Claudia sees is Paulo thrashing towards the steps, the Grand Canal flooding out of his Chinos as he hauls himself up. He offers his hand but she pushes it away and flounders around in the water while he leaps up the steps, grinning at his gob-smacked audience. At the top he strips off his shirt and makes a play of shaking himself dry like a dog. Claudia splutters up to the terrazzo, begins to yell, and yell, and around her everyone goes quiet and she hates it but can't stop it, the yelling sprays out of her mouth in a dirty stream until she's purged, drained, empty and Paulo is still smiling and playing to the crowd, pulling her into a clinch again, his dumb, bullish face too close, the grappa fumes hot and sour on his breath, the hellish stink of history pouring out of them both.

Some other books published by **Luath Press**

Selected Stories

Dilys Rose

1 84282 077 X PB £7.99

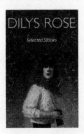

Selected Stories is a compelling compilation by the award-winning Scottish writer Dilys Rose, selected from her three previous books. Told from a wide range of perspectives and set in many parts of the world, Rose examines everyday lives on the edge through an unforgettable cast of characters. With subtlety, wit and dark humour, she demonstrates her seemingly effortless command of the short story form at every twist and turn of these deftly poised and finely crafted stories.

Praise for Rose's other work:

Dilys Rose can be compared to Katherine Mansfield in the way she takes hold of life and exposes all its vital elements in a few pages.
TIMES LITERARY SUPPLEMENT

Although Dilys Rose makes writing look effortless, make no mistake, to do so takes talent, skill and effort.
THE HERALD

The true short-story skills of empathy and cool, resonant economy shine through them all. Subtle excellence.
THE SCOTSMAN

Outlandish Affairs

Edited by Evan Rosenthal and Amanda Robinson

1 84282 055 9 PB £9.99

A plethora of bizarre and unusual questions arise when writers from both sides of the Atlantic – inspired by the multicultural nature of society – try to tackle the age old question of love.

When is a country singer gay and when is he straight?

Have you ever truly loved a seal?

Will *West Side Story* inspire the music of love to blossom?

Does an Icelandic strongman, semi-naked in a New York diner, do it for you?

Can Saddam Hussein be Prince Charming?

Have you ever dated anyone from another country, culture, world?

And if so, did sparks fly?

Discover in these stories what might happen when amorous encounters cross boundaries.

The Blue Moon Book

Anne MacLeod

1 84282 061 3 PB £9.99

Love can leave you breathless, lost for words.

Jess Kavanagh knows. Doesn't know. Twenty four hours after meeting and falling for archaeologist and Pictish expert Michael Hurt she suffers a horrific accident that leaves her with aphasia and amnesia. No words. No memory of love.

Michael travels south, unknowing. It is her estranged partner sports journalist Dan MacKie who is at the bedside when Jess finally regains consciousness. Dan, forced to review their shared past, is disconcerted by Jess's fear of him, by her loss of memory, loss of words.

Will their relationship survive this test? Should it survive? Will Michael find Jess again? In this absorbing contemporary novel, Anne MacLeod interweaves themes of language, love and loss in patterns as intricate, as haunting as the Pictish Stones.

High on drama and pathos, woven through with fine detail.
THE HERALD

The Glasgow Dragon

Des Dillon

1 84282 056 7 PB £9.99

What do I want?
Let me see now.
I want to destroy you spiritually, emotionally and mentally before I destroy you physically.

When Christie Devlin goes into business with a triad to take control of the Glasgow drug market, little does he know that his downfall and the destruction of his family is being plotted. As Devlin struggles with his own demons the real fight is just beginning. There are some things you should never forgive yourself for. Will he unlock the memories of the past in time to understand what is happening? Will he be able to save his daughter from the danger he has put her in? Nothing is as simple as good and evil.

Des Dillon is a master story-teller and this is a world he knows well. The authenticity, brutality, humour and most of all the humanity of the characters and the reality of the world they inhabit in Des Dillon's stories are never in question
LESLEY BENZIE

It has been known for years that Des Dillon writes some of Scotland's most vibrant prose ALAN BISSETT

Des Dillon's exuberant mastery of language energises everything he writes
JANET PAISLEY

Heartland

John MacKay
1 84282 059 1 PB £9.99

This was his land. He had sprung from it and would return surely to it. Its pure air refreshed him, the big skies inspired him and the pounding seas were the rhythm of his heart. It was his touchstone. Here he renourished his soul.

A man tries to build for his future by reconnecting with his past, leaving behind the ruins of the life he has lived. Iain Martin hopes that by returning to his Hebridean roots and embarking on a quest to reconstruct the ancient family home, he might find new purpose.

But as Iain begins working on the old blackhouse, he uncovers a secret from the past, which forces him to question everything he ever thought to be true.

Who can he turn to without betraying those to whom he is closest? His ailing mother, his childhood friend and his former love are both the building – and stumbling – blocks to his new life.

Where do you seek sanctuary when home has changed and will never be the same again?

Heartland *will hopefully keep readers turning the pages. It is built on an exploration of the ties to people and place, and of knowing who you are.*
JOHN MACKAY

Torch

Lin Anderson
1 84282 042 7 PB £9.99

Arson-probably the easiest crime to commit and the most difficult to solve.

When a young homeless girl dies in an arson attack on an empty building on Edinburgh's famous Princes Street, forensic scientist Rhona MacLeod is called over from Glasgow to help find the arsonist. Severino MacRae, half Scottish/half Italian and all misogynist, has other ideas. As Chief Fire Investigator, this is his baby and he doesn't want help - especially from a woman. Sparks fly when Rhona and Severino meet, but Severino's reluctance to involve Rhona may be more about her safety than his prejudice. As Hogmany approaches, Rhona and Severino play cat and mouse with an arsonist who will stop at nothing to gain his biggest thrill yet.

The second novel in the Dr Rhona MacLeod series finds this ill-matched pair's investigation take them deep into Edinburgh's sewers – but who are they up against? As the clock counts down to midnight, will they find out in time?

I just couldn't put it down. It's a real page-turner, a nail-biter – and that marvellous dialogue only a script-writer could produce. The plot, the Edinburgh atmosphere was spot on – hope that Rhona and Severino are to meet again – the sparks really fly there.
ALANNA KNIGHT

FICTION

Six Black Candles
Des Dillon
ISBN 1 84282 053 2 PB £6.99

Me and Ma Gal
Des Dillon
ISBN 1 84282 054 0 PB £5.99

The Kitty Killer Cult
Nick Smith
ISBN 1 84282 039 7 PB £9.99

Driftnet
Lin Anderson
ISBN 1 84282 034 6 PB £9.99

The Fundamentals of New Caledonia
David Nicol
ISBN 1 84282 93 6 HB £16.99

Milk Treading
Nick Smith
ISBN 1 84282 037 0 PB £6.99

The Road Dance
John MacKay
ISBN 1 84282 024 9 PB £6.99

The Strange Case of RL Stevenson
Richard Woodhead
ISBN 0 946487 86 3 HB £16.99

But n Ben A-Go-Go
Matthew Fitt
ISBN 0 946487 82 0 HB £10.99
ISBN 1 84282 014 1 PB £6.99

The Bannockburn Years
William Scott
ISBN 0 946487 34 0 PB £7.95

POETRY

Burning Whins
Liz Niven
ISBN 1 84282 074 5 PB £8.99

Drink the Green Fairy
Brian Whittingham
ISBN 1 84282 020 6 PB £8.99

Tartan & Turban
Bashabi Fraser
ISBN 1 84282 044 3 PB £8.99

The Ruba'iyat of Omar Khayyam, in Scots
Rab Wilson
ISBN 1 84282 046 X PB £8.99

Talking with Tongues
Brian D. Finch
ISBN 1 84282 006 0 PB £8.99

Kate o Shanter's Tale and other poems
Matthew Fitt
1 84282 028 1 PB £6.99 (book)
1 84282 043 5 £9.99 (audio CD)

Bad Ass Raindrop
Kokumo Rocks
ISBN 1 84282 018 4 PB £6.99

Madame Fifi's Farewell and other poems
Gerry Cambridge
ISBN 1 84282 005 2 PB £8.99

Poems to be Read Aloud
introduced by Tom Atkinson
ISBN 0 946487 00 6 PB £5.00

Scots Poems to be Read Aloud
introduced by Stuart McHardy
ISBN 0 946487 81 2 PB £5.00

Picking Brambles
Des Dillon
ISBN 1 84282 021 4 PB £6.99

Sex, Death & Football
Alistair Findlay
ISBN 1 84282 022 2 PB £6.99

The Luath Burns Companion
John Cairney
ISBN 1 84282 000 1 PB £10.00

Immortal Memories: A Compilation of Toasts to the Memory of Burns as delivered at Burns Suppers, 1801–2001
John Cairney
ISBN 1 84282 009 5 HB £20.00

The Whisky Muse: Scotch whisky in poem & song
Robin Laing
ISBN 1 84282 041 9 PB £7.99

A Long Stride Shortens the Road
Donald Smith
ISBN 1 84282 073 7 PB £8.99

Into the Blue Wavelengths
Roderick Watson
ISBN 1 84282 075 3 PB £8.99

The Souls of the Dead are Taking the Best Seats: 50 World Poets on War
Compiled by Angus Calder and Beth Junor
ISBN 1 84282 032 X PB £7.99

Sun Behind the Castle
Angus Calder
ISBN 1 84282 078 8 PB £8.99

THE QUEST FOR

The Quest for the Celtic Key
Karen Ralls-MacLeod and Ian Robertson
1 84282 084 2 PB £7.99

The Quest for the Nine Maidens
Stuart McHardy
ISBN 0 946487 66 9 HB £16.99

The Quest for Charles Rennie Mackintosh
John Cairney
ISBN 1 84282 058 3 HB £16.99

The Quest for Robert Louis Stevenson
John Cairney
ISBN 1 84282 085 0 PB £8.99

The Quest for the Original Horse Whisperers
Russell Lyon
ISBN 1 84282 020 6 HB £16.99

The Quest for Arthur
Stuart McHardy
ISBN 1 84282 012 5 HB £16.99

ON THE TRAIL OF

On the Trail of Mary Queen of Scots
J. Keith Cheetham
ISBN 0 946487 50 2 PB £7.99

On the Trail of William Wallace
David R. Ross
ISBN 0 946487 47 2 PB £7.99

On the Trail of Robert the Bruce
David R. Ross
ISBN 0 946487 52 9 PB £7.99

On the Trail of Robert Service
GW Lockhart
ISBN 0 946487 24 3 PB £7.99

On the Trail of Robert Burns
John Cairney
ISBN 0 946487 51 0 PB £7.99

On the Trail of Bonnie Prince Charlie
David R Ross
ISBN 0 946487 68 5 PB £7.99

On the Trail of Queen Victoria in the Highlands
Ian R Mitchell
ISBN 0 946487 79 0 PB £7.99

LANGUAGE

Luath Scots Language Learner
L Colin Wilson
ISBN 0 946487 91 X PB £9.99 (book)
ISBN 1 84282 026 5 CD £16.99 (double audio CD set)

Details of these and other Luath Press titles are to be found at www.luath.co.uk

Luath Press Limited

committed to publishing well written books worth reading

LUATH PRESS takes its name from Robert Burns, whose little collie Luath
(*Gael.*, swift or nimble) tripped up Jean Armour at a wedding and gave
him the chance to speak to the woman who was to be his wife and the
abiding love of his life. Burns called one of *The Twa Dogs*
Luath after Cuchullin's hunting dog in *Ossian's Fingal*.
Luath Press was established in 1981 in the heart of
Burns country, and is now based a few steps up
the road from Burns' first lodgings on
Edinburgh's Royal Mile. Luath offers you
distinctive writing with a hint of
unexpected pleasures.

Most bookshops in the UK, the US, Canada,
Australia, New Zealand and parts of Europe,
either carry our books in stock or can order them
for you. To order direct from us, please send a £sterling
cheque, postal order, international money order or your
credit card details (number, address of cardholder and
expiry date) to us at the address below. Please add post
and packing as follows: UK – £1.00 per delivery address;
overseas surface mail – £2.50 per delivery address; overseas airmail –
£3.50 for the first book to each delivery address, plus £1.00 for each
additional book by airmail to the same address. If your order is a gift, we
will happily enclose your card or message at no extra charge.

Luath Press Limited
543/2 Castlehill
The Royal Mile
Edinburgh EH1 2ND
Scotland
Telephone: 0131 225 4326 (24 hours)
Fax: 0131 225 4324
email: gavin.macdougall@luath. co.uk
Website: www. luath.co.uk